Copyright © 2017 by Ashe Moon

2023 - 2nd Edition

All rights reserved. No part of this publication may be reproduced, distributed, or transmitted in any form or by any means, including photocopying, recording, or other electronic or mechanical methods, without the prior written permission of the publisher, except in the case of brief quotations embodied in critical reviews and certain other noncommercial uses permitted by copyright law.

DOCTOR TO THE OMEGA

THE LUNA BROTHERS MPREG ROMANCE SERIES

Stay updated with sales and new releases by subscribing to Ashe Moon's personal newsletter! Scan the QR code below with your phone camera!

* * *

If you're looking for something a little more personal you can also join my private Facebook group, **Ashe Moon's Ashetronauts**!

My group is a safe space to chat with me and other readers, and where I also do special exclusive giveaways and announcements. Hope to see you there!

THE LUNA BROTHERS SERIES

Loch's Story - Wed to the Omega
Christophe's Story - Marked to the Omega
Arthur's Story - Bound to the Omega

VANDER

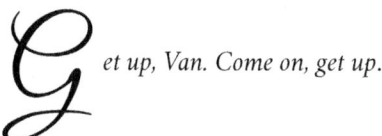 *et up, Van. Come on, get up.*

The dark, sticky mud grabbed at my body, pulling me downwards with every attempt I made to get to back up. All around me, bare feet, boots, and wolf paws beat into the mud, showering me with the thick black grime as freezing raindrops drummed down onto my fur. I got one paw up, then another, then another, the world whirling around me as I tried to get my head straight. I'd taken a pretty nasty tumble getting down the shattered boulder obstacle, and I was pretty sure that I was bleeding from somewhere on my head. I could smell the blood, and I tasted it on my muzzle. Or was it someone else's? I didn't know.

Finally, I managed to get to my feet. I looked over my shoulder at the mass of towering, ragged granite boulders that were piled up three stories into the mud, and saw the remaining stragglers trying to navigate their way down without losing their footing. The people who had decided to stay in their human or half-wolf forms were obviously having the hardest time—they were trying to lower themselves down, or were slipping off the slick rocks when they tried to jump down. I winced as one trainee lost his grip and fell to the mud ten feet below him. He groaned and struggled to get up—his hind leg had snapped. He reached down with his snout and tore the rescue beacon off from the strap around his waist and activated it. It sent a flash of brilliant red light into the air, calling in a healing evac team. That was it—activate your beacon and you're out of the run.

I was already so far behind. If I wasn't within the first thirty people to finish the entrance course, I could say goodbye to my shot at being accepted into the Fighting Arts School. Only the strongest got into the FAS.

I already had a big handicap—I was an omega. Training to be a master fighter was typically an alpha's field. Betas weren't even allowed to do it—they were too weak—but omegas were special. We had the potential to be stronger than betas, and sometimes we could even match or exceed alphas in strength.

Sometimes.

I'd always dreamed that I would get into the FAS, just like my alpha older brother, Loch. I was so convinced that I would have what it took. Loch's husband, Tresten, was an omega, and was well on his way to receiving the rank of master. Seeing his strength pushed me forward. My father was a strong fighter, as well as my brother and my brother-in-law. I was so convinced that I was strong, that I got into a fight about it with some piece of dog shit at school. He and his buddies put me in the hospital. That probably should've been a wakeup call for me.

Now, as I crawled bleeding in the mud, desperately trying to claw my way back up to the first thirty, I realized that I wasn't one of those omegas. I wasn't like Tresten, not at all.

A helicopter roared overhead, a camera peering down over the obstacle course and broadcasting the event to the audience watching it in the stands on distant edge of the gigantic arena. This place was old—even older than the Dawn Academy, the college that the Fighting Arts School was a part of. Over many generations, thousands of entrance trials had been run in this massive space. I'd been told that a long time ago, the trials were even tougher—deaths were practically guaranteed.

Today, it was practically a spectator sport. The families and friends of the hopefuls made up the audience in the stands, but people also watched it live in their homes. They were all eager to see who would make up the newest class at the FAS—some of whom might end up becoming famous fighters. After all, the Dawn Academy was *the* most prestigious wolf college in this part of the world. Only the best, brightest and wealthiest went to school there.

. . .

There was one wolf who I knew would be at the front of the pack. His name was Lex Wolfbridge, and he was the hottest alpha I'd ever laid my eyes on. I'd gone to high school with him, and I had a *huge* crush on him. He was a certified genius fighter, top of the class and a shoo-in for the Fighting Arts School. Getting into the FAS had always been my goal ever since I was a kid, and knowing Lex would be going there was only more motivation for me to be accepted too. Sure, the guy barely knew I existed—it was only after I got my ass kicked and sent to the hospital that he seemed to notice me out of pity—but I'd take what I could get, and before this day in hell began, Lex came to *me* and wished me good luck.

It was the thought of his perfect face that pushed me forward now, urging me through each grueling obstacle.

Come on, Van. Faster. Don't you want to get into the FAS so you can train with Lex? If you get in, he'll notice you. You can be his...

The grey winter rainclouds overhead slowly turned dark until they became storm clouds. The rain pelted down even harder, and I heard the rumbling of thunder from somewhere in the distance. I bolted ahead, the thick mud transitioning into bog and high grass. I could see trails cut into the reeds from where the faster runners had entered into the marsh, which stretched out on either side of me for what seemed like miles. The ones who were even slower than me were still coming up behind me through the mud, and some were also entering the bog. I spotted Kris Lanford, another alpha I went to school with. He had always been one of the weaker students, and right now he looked fucking ragged, his entire wolf body caked with heavy mud. If I was running alongside Kris, then I had to be *really* behind.

I pushed forward into the thick reeds, shifting from my full wolf form to my half-wolf. I needed to be on two feet to navigate through this muck. I quickly realized that following any of the tracks and paths would be pointless—they crisscrossed all over without any specific direction. It was obvious that some people had had no idea which way to take through the nearly shoulder-high grass.

I sniffed the air, trying to get a sense of my bearings. I knew that past the bog was the final obstacle—a large lake that we needed to cross—so I tried to smell for a whiff of fresh water. The rain was freezing and made it hard to separate the sharp, murky scent of the bog from anything else. I pushed forward, hoping I was going the right way, my nose turned up to the wind. Red beams were flashing up all around me now—people lost in the bog. Thunder boomed closer just as a rescue helicopter buzzed overhead, lowering down two halfwolf shifted healers into the tall grass. After a minute they lifted back out, a lost and shivering runner strapped to them. The helicopter pulled away and flew off to the location of the next closest beacon.

Suddenly, I caught the scent I'd been searching for. It was faint, but it was there. *Fresh water*. It was a good thing too, because I'd been running in the completely wrong direction. I turned to my left and kept my nose to the air, doing my best to keep the scent locked in. I was so close now. Could I make it within the first thirty? I had no idea, but given how many people seemed to be getting lost in the bog and extracted, maybe I actually had a chance. I wondered where Lex was. Knowing him, probably already finished. An image of him being fawned over by a group of girls and omegas—my competition—flashed through my head and urged me forward. I wanted to him to see how strong I could be. I wanted so badly for him to recognize me and give me a chance. I wanted him to see me and tell me how wonderful I was.

"Hey, would you want to get together sometime? We're going to be training together. You could come over to my place, and I could show you some techniques..." That was exactly what I wanted him to say to me.

I can do it, I thought. *I can make it. I can—*

My fantasy was cut short. I fell straight down, my snout slamming straight down into the murky bog water. *My feet were trapped!* I resisted panic and pushed myself upright, sputtering out the rank water from nose. I'd been trapped in some kind of underwater quicksand and was quickly sinking down. The water was nearing my waist, and had completely submerged my tail. I struggled to pull my legs free, but even with the extra strength that my half-wolf form gave me, I couldn't get free.

Now the panic was setting in. I continued to see the flashes of red light shooting up into the sky and realized that people weren't getting lost, they were getting *stuck*, just like I was. I thrashed, straining against the sucking mud to get my legs free, but every time I moved it seemed to pull me down even quicker. The water was pushing past my abs now. My hand went to my waist where my beacon was strapped. One click of the button and it was all over—I'd be safe, but I could say goodbye to the FAS.

No. It's not over yet. Don't panic, calm down.

I thought back to the advice that my brother-in-law, Tresten, gave to me before the trials.

"Keep your center. Keep balanced. If you rely too much on your emotions, you'll find yourself in trouble. Take a moment to calm yourself and think."

There was no way I could lift my legs free from the mud. In my half-wolf form, I was too large and heavy, and any attempt would just pull me in deeper. No, I would need to make myself smaller...

Closing my eyes, I began the shift back to human form. My body shrunk down, my wolf ears pulling back to the sides of my head, my snout pulling inwards. I could feel the mud loosening around my legs as they grew smaller, but at the same time, the water level was rising even higher as I became shorter. It was up to my neck now, and soon it'd be covering my head. I had one shot at this...

. . .

I took in a deep breath and dropped my head below the water, leaning forward to drop my hands to the ground. Then I pushed.

The soil was much more compact where my hands were. I pushed with my forearms and my elbows and clawed at the mud as I wriggled my legs. I pulled and pushed, until finally...

I exploded up above the water, gasping for breath. *Freedom!*

There was no time to celebrate. I continued forward, wading through the chest-high water in my human form. I wouldn't be able to see above the grass, but there was less of a chance of getting stuck in another sinkhole. I shifted out just enough, targeting my ears and nose so that I could gain the extra sensory abilities of my wolf and follow the trail to the final obstacle. Being in my human form, I was naked except for the pair of skin-tight underwear that made transitioning between forms easy.

I was freezing. The winter rain continued to beat down, and the marsh water was a numbing cold. I pushed on, fighting the mud from sucking me down. Then my ears pricked up with the sound of raindrops pattering on open water, and the scent of fresh water became strong. I moved faster, the thick grass and reeds cutting at my bare skin as my breath formed puffs of white on the frigid air. *Come on, come on.* How far away was I? How big was this bog? I had a sudden image of myself going the wrong direction again, moving parallel to the water, never making it out. A surge of desperation hit me. I was frantic, and the tall grass seemed to get even thicker. I could feel the weight of my rescue beacon on my hip, below the surface of the water. All it took was one press, and I'd be out of here.

And then, finally, I broke through.

The grass opened into a stretch of dark water, and on the distant, opposite shore I could see the lights of the finish line. I could just make up out the shapes of people there—the hopefuls who had completed their run and were being tended to by healers and family who had been transported in from the spectator area. In my mind's eye, I imagined Lex over there, looking out over the water. I pictured myself emerging from the lake, tired but triumphant, and him coming over to give me a proud hug.

"I knew you could do it," he might say to me.

There was a sign at the edge of the water with the number "24" glowing on it. It suddenly ticked to "25", and I realized what it meant.

I wasn't too late. There were still 5 more spaces left—but there wouldn't be for long. I could see the shapes of several people swimming through the water towards the finish in the distance, two of which shot up a red rescue beacon. Then I sensed a presence to my right, and was surprised to see Kris

Lanford emerge from the grass. He looked at me, and then splashed forward into the lake and started to swim. *Shit.* I dove in and started to swim as fast as I could.

The water was even icier than what was in the swamp. It stabbed at my skin like thousands of fangs, making every second torture. There was a bright flash followed seconds later by the loudest bang I'd ever heard as lightning struck somewhere off in the not so distant distance. I nearly choked on the water in terror, and wondered if maybe the lightning had struck someone swimming. *This is not good.* I was thrumming with adrenaline and fear, and fought to keep my concentration. In my mind, I conjured an image of my goal— *get into the FAS. You're almost there. Just keep swimming.*

I was doing everything I could not to panic, not to succumb to the terror that was gripping me. I could feel the cold seeping into my legs and making my bones ache along where'd they been fractured during the beating that'd put me in the hospital. I wondered if they might give out at any moment. It'd been two years since that'd happened. My body was fully healed by now. *Wasn't it?* Would I suddenly lock up, lose all control of myself and die drowning in this freezing water?

Just keep swimming. It was all I could do, because I sure as hell was *not* going to get pulled out of here.

I locked my eyes on the glowing orange counter off in the distance. It seemed so damn far away.

Come on, Van. Come on.

The rain blurred my vision, and it felt like it was doing its best to push me under the water with its hard and heavy droplets. I could barely see anything, the numbers becoming nothing but spots of light that served as a last bastion of motivation.

Almost there.

"Help!"

At first I thought the garbled voice was a hallucination induced by the biting cold water, but then I heard it again.

"Vander! Help me!"

I looked to the source of the voice and saw Kris straining to keep his head above the water.

"Vander, help! Over here! Help! I'm sinking!"

"Use your beacon!" I shouted to him. "Pull out!"

"My hands," he yelled. "My arms. Cramping. I can't..."

His face slipped beneath the surface.

Shit.

Out of the corner of my eye, back towards the bog, more runners emerged and dove into the lake. I saw the sign tick from 26 to 27. I wanted to keep going. I was so close. A part of me was drawn by the call to glory—*swim on, you're almost there.*

I turned away from the sign and swam as quickly as I could to where Kris had disappeared. I took a deep breath and went below the surface, the icy water clawing at my face and my open eyes. I saw Kris gliding down toward the dark depths, his face turned up at me, his eyes wide with fear. A mass of bubbles exploded out from his nose and mouth as he let out his breath. I kicked my legs as hard as I could, reached out with my hands... and grabbed him. I turned back towards the surface, but the guy was dragging me back down. He was dead weight in the water, and there was no way I could get him to the surface on my own. He was going to die if I didn't do something—the one thing that I could do.

I reached down and ripped the rescue beacon from my waist, activating its brilliant red light. The beam cut through the murky water and erupted from the surface—I could tell it was shining straight up into the sky. *Hurry*, I thought. My lungs were on fire, and all I could do was hope that Kris was still hanging on.

Hurry.

We were sinking down, my legs numb and unable to move. I squeezed my arm around Kris's waist and held my other hand as high above me as I could. Everything was closing around me, going black as my lungs screamed for air…

I felt powerful arms wrap around me. Kris was yanked away, and I tore through the water and broke the surface. An alpha bear shifter looked down at me as he pulled me onto a life raft. I saw the whirling blades of the rescue helicopter up above us. To my left, I saw an alpha in half-wolf shift lifting Kris onto the raft. "This one isn't responding," he said. "Attempting resuscitation."

"Can you hear me?" my rescuer bellowed at me.

I coughed and greedily drew air into my starved lungs, nodding. "Yes," I breathed. "I can… keep going."

He shook his head. "There's no way I'm putting you back in that water. You're going to freeze to death or die from the shock. You're done, kid." He wrapped me up in a silver emergency blanket and waved his hand up at the helicopter, and I felt the raft lift from the surface of the water.

. . .

"No," I murmured. "Please…"

"Don't worry," the rescue healer said. "We're getting you out of here."

I closed my eyes, and my world went black.

* * *

When I came back to consciousness, the helicopter had landed and the team of three healers were carrying me on a stretcher. I looked over and saw Kris being carried too, an oxygen mask placed over his mouth. His team separated from me, taking him off somewhere else.

They carried me into a large tent that was bustling with people. Looking around, I could see that it was mixed with people who had finished the trials, and those who had called for rescue but were in good health. Everyone was talking, congratulating one another, and greeting their family members as uniformed workers served hot drinks. I could see that the majority of the finishers were within the top thirty, designated by a golden medal placed around their necks with their completion number etched into it.

"You're awake," the bear who'd pulled me out of the water said. He was back in his human form, but I recognized his ruby eyes. He was tall, with a stocky, muscular build that was typical of bear alphas. He had dark brown hair, and wore a short beard that framed a serious face. I had to admit—the guy was really good looking. I hadn't had many encounters with bears—wolves didn't mix with them often, and I'd gone to all wolf schools my entire life. From everything I'd been told by my parents and my friends, bears were simple and rural folk who cared more about bumming around in the woods than anything else.

"You did a very brave thing," he said. "You saved his life, you know. He would've drowned if you hadn't come for him."

"How many are left?" I asked, ignoring what he'd said.

"How many?"

"In the trial."

"There's still about eighty or so left, I think. When we pulled you out, the counter was at 33."

I sighed, covering my eyes with the back of my hand.

"Here, sit up," he said, helping me upright. "We've notified your family, they'll be here soon."

. . .

I got to my feet, and one of the other healers handed me a clean set of robes with the Dawn Academy sigil embroidered on them. I dropped the emergency blanket and wrapped myself up in the robes. Seeing the sigil over my heart would've filled me with pride and excitement, but now knowing that I would not be making it into the school it only made me feel like a fake.

"I was so fucking close," I muttered. "I can't believe it."

"Don't be so hard on yourself," he said calmly. "You demonstrated real bravery out there. As far as I'm concerned, that's something to be proud of."

"I just did what I needed to," I said.

"I know how important these trials are to you wolf fighters," he said. "And I know for a fact that many would've blindly gone ahead towards the finish line, hoping to make it under that thirty. I've been a rescue healer at thirteen trials, and I've seen it every time. I don't think I'll ever understand that blind selfishness that wolves have. Such dedication to something that only hurts other people."

"Fighters *protect*," I said. "We're not selfish. We keep our clans and families safe. What do bears do?"

. . .

He gave me an apologetic smile. "I'm sorry, I didn't mean to offend you." He packed up the stretcher and his healer kit. "But really, kid, risking your life like that is evidence enough that you've got guts. If it were my decision, I'd say what you did was good enough to get you into the FAS."

"Thanks," I said dejectedly.

He eyed me. "You ever thought about becoming a rescue healer?"

I laughed. "Not once."

"Well, maybe you should. You've got the spirit."

"That's alright."

He shrugged. "Think about it. If using your abilities to save lives sounds like something you'd want to do..." He produced a small white business card and handed it to me. "Come find me."

"Doctor Pell Darkclaw, North Forest Evergreen Clan," the card said, and below that, *"Rescue and Healing Technician, Heli-Hound Rescue Inc."*

. . .

"Right," I said, slipping the card into the inner pocket of the robe.

He and his team left, leaving me to my thoughts and the bustle of the tent. The celebrations around me were raucous. Groups of alphas jumped around, proudly showing off their gold completion medals. Slowly, more and more sullen, exhausted and defeated losers began to file in.

"I was so close," I heard someone say. "Number 46."

You were close? I *was close*. I could've made it.

I could feel the strain of the day finally creeping over my body. I don't know if I'd ever worked my body so hard in my entire life. I made my way over to the refreshments table to drink some water and eat something. As I grabbed a bottle of water and munched on a protein bar, I became aware that I was being looked at. I knew exactly why—it'd happened in the staging area before the trials had started, too. It was because I was an omega. In fact, I was pretty sure I was the only omega competing this year.

Tresten had warned me this would happen, but even so, I couldn't help but feel slightly unnerved by it. I'd never been in an alpha-dominated environment like this, and it was intimidating.

. . .

I concentrated on my snack, trying to filter out the constant gleam of red alpha eyes that were glancing my way. That's when I spotted him.

Lex was chatting with a group of other sub-thirty finishers, an easy grin on his perfect face. He looked flawless, like he'd just done the easiest thing in the world. His hair was damp and brushed back, as if he'd just stepped out of the shower. His spotless appearance was a definite contrast to my crusty, mud-splattered body. I picked a piece of grass from my hair and tried to gather my courage. I had to at least say something to Lex.

I took a deep breath and strode over to him, fighting the urge to melt into a quivering blob at his feet.

"Hi, Lex," I said, my voice cracking. I winced, cleared my throat and smiled at him as he turned to look at me and frowned.

"Vander?" He started to laugh. "Wow, you look like shit."

I gaped at him.

"Just fucking around with you," he said.

. . .

"Oh," I replied, slightly stunned. "Um… I just wanted to tell you, congratulations. I knew you'd get in the top thirty."

One of his alpha companions snorted. "Top thirty? Lex was the *first* to finish the course. Nobody can touch him."

"Wow," I beamed. "That's incredible, Lex!"

"Yeah," he agreed. "It was nothing." He turned away to talk to one of his friends.

"Um," I piped up. "I nearly finished in the top thirty too. Your encouragement meant a lot to me."

"Encouragement?"

"Yes," I nodded. "When you wished me good luck."

"Oh," he said. "You didn't finish, though. I guess it wasn't enough, then." His friends laughed, and I tried to laugh along, feeling self-conscious.

"I would've made it," I explained. "I nearly did. But someone needed my help. In the lake, they were drowning, so I turned back to save them. I managed to get to them, and had to use my rescue beacon to get him out of there."

. . .

"You mean, you sacrificed your shot at finishing to save them?" Lex asked.

"Yeah," I said, straightening up. Speaking about it out loud, I did feel proud of what I'd done. The bear's words repeated in my mind— *"that is evidence enough that you've got the guts to be in the FAS."*

"Man," he said, a puzzled look on his face. "I bet you wish you hadn't. I woudln't have..."

Numbness sank into me, like I was slowly being lowered back into that freezing lake. I had not expected him to respond that way.

"I-I... what? No..."

But he had already turned back to his friends. I felt shocked, like he had just slapped me in the face, and in that moment the impossible happened—I felt all the attraction I had for Lex Wolfbridge evaporating away.

I slunk away to an isolated corner of the tent and sat down on a folding chair. The space was starting to fill up as more runners completed the trial and more families arrived to greet them. As upset as I was about Lex's coldness, I was more disturbed about my own feelings about it. Yes, I'd turned around to save Kris, but there was a brief moment as I was challenged with the decision where I *did* think about leaving him there. The pull of making it across the finish under the top thirty was so strong. It was my dream, after all.

Was the FAS really worth sacrificing a fellow wolf for?

"Van!"

I looked up and saw my family walking towards me, with my favorite older brother, Loch, leading the way. He held his son, my little three-year-old nephew, Ian, in his arms. Tresten, his husband, walked beside him, and behind them were the rest of my family: Christophe, my eldest brother, Arthur, the second eldest, and my mother and father.

"What a relief that you're safe," Mom said. "We saw you on the screen. When you went under the water after that boy, I nearly had a heart attack."

"Don't be disappointed," said Dad. "It wasn't your fault. You were extremely close."

"You fought hard," Loch said. "You have nothing to be ashamed of."

"That's right," said Mom. "The Dawn Academy has plenty of other good programs…"

. . .

I stood up. "Can we go?"

Dad frowned. "Go now? There's still the closing ceremony."

"What does it matter? It's meaningless for me. I didn't even finish."

"Well," Dad went on, "I'd like to chat with my old friends after the ceremony, and…"

I pushed past them, hot tears welling up in my eyes. *Why am I crying? Am I just that weak? A weak little omega not hard enough to survive in the world of the fighters.*

"Vander!" I heard Dad shout. I flinched, but didn't stop.

"Let him be," Mom said, her voice trailing away as I disappeared into the thickening crowd until I escaped out of the tent into the cold winter night, and was immediately soaked by the pouring rain. A streak of lightning cracked off in the distance. I walked against the flow of people heading up the path towards the tent, heading nowhere in particular. I just needed to get away from everyone.

. . .

What if I hadn't turned around? What if I'd gone straight on and made it to the finish? I would've made it. I might've even gotten Lex to notice my abilities. Maybe he and I would've had a chance...

I shivered, a wave of revulsion washing over me. I saw Kris's face in my mind, the way he looked at me with those terrified eyes as he sank down into the darkness.

The was no *way* I could've let him drown, and knowing that Lex would've made me want to puke. And what about my brother? My father? What would they have done?

The rain started pattering onto an umbrella that had been held over my head, and I turned to see that Tresten had come up beside me. "Hi, Van," he said.

"Hey, Tresten. Did they send you out after me?"

"I volunteered," he said.

We stood in silence for a while, until I finally spoke up.

"What would you have done?" I asked. "In the lake."

. . .

He thought about my question for a long time. "My father taught me that the purpose of fighting is to protect and save lives, and with that I guess I would've done what you did. But I also know the blinding obsession of being accepted into the FAS. I know the feeling of being willing to die for it, and to sacrifice everything else for it. That's the kind of emotion that the Fighting Arts School wants in its students. They want their fighters to be able to sacrifice everything for their art, so that in battle they can fight without fear of anything at all."

"So, I'm really just not cut out for this after all. I'm too weak."

Tresten shook his head. "What you need to understand is that the FAS isn't the *only* way. I was lucky to have my father to give me that lesson. To keep me balanced. Without balance, we'll destroy ourselves. Being that cold, that ruthless, you'll become a machine, and machines are easily broken and dismantled. You took a different path to strength today."

"I… can't believe that so many fighters seem to have been willing to let Kris drown."

"Most of us were never put in the situation you were. I wasn't, Loch wasn't. If my father was, he never told me. People might say they would've done anything to gain entrance to the school, because they want to show that they're strong and have the mentality of a fighter—but if they were put in that situation, I think most would've done what you did. At least, that's what I'd like to believe."

"Van."

Tresten and I turned around to see Loch walking towards us. He held up an umbrella as their son Ian, who had shifted into his wolf-pup form, splashed around in the puddles. Tresten sighed and went to scoop him up. "You're going to get your fur all muddy," he scolded.

"Hey, Loch," I said, giving my brother a sorry smile.

"You alright?"

I nodded.

"It's not the end of the world—after all, you can always hold off starting school for a year and try again next year."

"I don't think I'll be trying again," I said.

Loch looked surprised. "Are you sure? Buddy, you've been ranting about the FAS for years. You're just going to give up? One extra year isn't going to put you far behind in training. I can help you train. So can Tresten."

"No," I said. "I don't know."

"You think about it," he said. "Don't let one failure get in the way of your dreams."

I told him I would—but the thing was that I was questioning everything I thought I knew about becoming a fighter. If I got into the Fighting Arts School, what sacrifices would I be asked to make? Who would I be forced to drown in the name of personal greatness?

* * *

Mom opened the door to my room, sending a slim triangle of light across the floor, and peeked her head inside. "Vander," she said. "Dinner is ready."

"Mm," I mumbled, turning over in bed.

She sighed and slowly closed the door, pulling darkness back over me. I heard quiet whispering outside of my door.

"He's been like this for two days," I heard her say.

"Give him time, Mother." It was Christophe, my eldest brother. He'd always been the voice of reason amongst our siblings—high achieving, refined, and our parent's favorite. I didn't much care for him, but I did appreciate him looking out for me right now.

"I just don't understand," Mom said, exasperatedly. "It's not the end of the world."

"I've been told that he was rejected by an alpha he was infatuated with, so on top of failing the trials…"

Ugh. How did he hear about *that*? Then again, it wasn't a surprise. Christophe was also nosy as hell.

"There's plenty more wolves in the pack," I heard Mom say before their voices faded away with their footsteps.

I sighed, pulled myself out of bed and went to the window. I felt lost. Nothing seemed to make sense anymore. I couldn't stop thinking about what Tresten had said to me the night of the trials—*the FAS isn't the only way. You took a different path to strength.*

What other way was there?

I slid out of bed and emerged from my bedroom to slowly make my way downstairs to where my family was eating dinner. Dad looked up from his plate of steak and gave me a rare smile. "Glad you could join us, Vander," he said.

I took my seat, and Tina, our housekeeper, came around with a plate of steak for me. "Thank you," I said quietly.

"How are you feeling?" Mom asked.

I nodded. "Better. I think I know what I need to do."

"Wonderful," she said, beaming. "I knew you'd figure it out. The Dawn Academy offers *so* many fantastic different areas of study that I *know* you can excel at…"

"No, Mom," I said. "I'm not going to go to Dawn."

Her mouth hung open wordlessly. "You're not?"

Dawn was my parent's alma mater—I knew it'd been their hope to see me there as much as it'd been mine.

"What is your plan, then?" Dad asked sternly. Christophe and Arthur both turned from their dinners to look at me, curious.

. . .

"I think… I need to do some searching," I said. "I need to get away and find some answers."

"You can go stay with Loch and Tresten," Mom said. "That would be a wonderful idea."

"I don't think he's talking about staying with Loch," said Arthur.

"What are you thinking, Van?" asked Dad. "What is your plan?"

"Go north, maybe," I said. "Hitchhike. Maybe walk."

Mom looked horrified. "North!"

"North," said Dad, stroking his chin.

"North?" laughed Christophe.

"North," Arthur said moonily. "That sounds exciting."

Mom glared at him. "I don't think it sounds exciting at all. I think it sounds dangerous for an omega. What's north? What can you find there that you couldn't find here? Stay with

Loch, go on a tour of the Dawn Academy. They have some wonderful intermediary programs you could try before it comes time to decide…"

"I think it's a good idea," Dad said, which surprised me—I was certain he'd be even more disapproving than Mom was. "An adventure into the unknown to build your strength and your confidence. The Lunas have been doing it for ages!"

"Really?" asked Arthur.

"Your grandfather traveled the world after he fought in the Clan War. He met all sorts of people, made many connections…"

"Isn't that when he got robbed and beaten up by hyena shifters and lost his memory for a month?" asked Christophe.

"Well, yes," said Dad. "But he got better, and when he came back he enrolled at the Dawn Academy's Business Arts School."

"Lost his memory?" Mom looked like she was going to faint. "I never heard about this story."

"I think it's a great idea," Dad said. "Go out and learn the ways of the world firsthand."

. . .

"What's north?" Mom asked, sounding a little frantic.

"Not much," said Christophe. "The Northern Forest. A few tiny towns. To be frank, *east* is probably more interesting. There isn't much up north."

"That's fine," I said. "I want to be somewhere alone where I can think."

In truth, I hadn't given my idea much thought at all—I'd practically pulled it out of my ass at that moment—but now that it was on the table, I was set on doing it. A journey of self-discovery was what I needed, and getting away from the world I'd known for my entire life was probably the best thing I could do.

And hell, maybe in one of those tiny northern towns I'd meet a sexy alpha wolf looking for a strong, city omega to be his mate.

PELL

"Is it bad, Doctor?"

Mrs. Windheart fidgeted with her purse, watching me as I inspected her son's arm. Cherry Windheart lived in Houndsville, just on the edge of the northern forest. She was a single mother, a beta wolf, and Rian, her little son, had a bad habit of getting hurt. Like most of residents of Houndsville, she was poor. Too poor to afford healing services in Wolfheart, the big wolf city down south. That was how things were up in the north; nothing like Wolfheart, where all the wealthiest wolf clans in the world lived and operated.

Like many bear shifters, I'd been raised with the thought that all wolves were greedy and violent, always trying to expand their territory to take what they could from the bear clans who lived peaceful, minimal lifestyles in the forests and mountains. At age twenty-one, I set out from my town to go south and find out for myself. What I discovered along the way was that most wolves were just like us—trying to find a way to live in this world.

I decided not to return to my town to find a mate after the typical five years of field training that bear healers went through. Instead, I decided to continue to work as a helicopter rescue healer in Wolfheart, and to live a solitary life in the Northern Forest. I worked at small healing clinics in each of the small towns that lay at the edge of the forest—Pinetown, Forest Ridge, and Houndsville. Occasionally, I returned back to Ursidcomb, my hometown up north, to check in with my parents, who always bugged me about coming back to find a mate.

"Find a nice girl or boy back home," they'd say. "Take over your father's practice."

"I don't want to find a nice girl or boy," I'd tell them. "I have my own work in the city. I'm taking care of people who need me. You should see the healers they have there. They need my skills."

"Wolves," my father would complain. "They're too dumb to tell their tail from their nose, how can they train competent healers?"

. . .

Eventually my mother would start to become emotional. "Don't tell me you'd rather be with a wolf girl! You've spent so much time in that city, my son is turning into a hound!"

It'd been two years since I'd been back home. I couldn't go back, not after what happened the last time.

I couldn't abide by what they wanted from me—settling down, taking over the practice, basically becoming the next version of them. I had people to take care of—the people of these towns, and the entire city of Wolfheart.

"Mrs. Windheart," I said, "Rian just has a sprained muscle. I'll give him a sling for it. He'll need to refrain from using it until it's healed, which should only be a few days. Luckily for little wolf boys like you, your body heals itself quickly. But Rian?"

He looked up at me sheepishly.

"Not using it means not running around in your wolf form. Understand?"

"Aww..."

"Don't grumble," his mother scolded. "Tell Dr. Darkclaw that you understand."

. . .

"I understand. I won't shift."

I smiled. "It'll only be a few days." I went into a drawer and found a simple fabric sling, and then showed his mother how to tie it onto him. "Please keep an eye on him, and come back in a week."

"Thank you, Doctor," she said, and then looked embarrassed. "How much will this visit cost me? I recently got paid…"

"It's just an examination. Nothing owed," I said.

"Oh, thank you…"

I led her out to the front of the clinic to make an appointment with the receptionist. The office was filled with patients waiting their turn, many of which I already knew by name.

"Dr. Darkclaw?" Rian said.

"What's up?"

"Can I see your ears?"

. . .

His mother looked embarrassed. "That's not something you ask someone, Rian," she said.

"No, it's fine," I said, laughing. A little wolf boy in a small town like this didn't often get a chance to meet a bear shifter. I crouched down, closed my eyes, and my bear ears popped up out of my hair on the top of my head. Rian giggled and reached out to feel them.

"They're so much fuzzier than wolf ears," he observed. "And round."

"Yes, they are," I said.

"They're funny. I like them."

"I like them too." I stood up, and Rian waved to me with his good arm. Mrs. Windheart gave me a thankful smile.

I quickly worked my way through the remaining patients and then left for the nearby town of Forest Ridge. Shifting into my bear form, I could reach Forest Ridge from Houndsville running at a brisk sprint in a matter of an hour. The sky was shaded with a haze of grey clouds, and from the smell of the air I could tell that it was going to snow within the next day or two.

. . .

The tiny clinic at Forest Ridge was also packed with people waiting their turn to be seen. I greeted the ones I knew and made my way into the back, where Dr. Helena Elpaw was treating a patient. Dr. Elpaw was an alpha female wolf, and the owner of the three clinics I volunteered my time at. I'd met her through my rescue healer job—she was a graduate of the Healing Arts School at the Dawn Academy in Wolfheart, was extremely wealthy, and was also one of the most generous, philanthropic people I knew.

"Good morning, Dr. Darkclaw," she said, her face set in its trademark serious expression. "Everything in order in Houndsville?"

"Mr. Kellings is back with the paw condition. Ms. Firetooth has a bad cold, I gave her some medication. Mrs. Windheart's son, Rian, sprained his arm."

"Mm," she said, and turned back to her patient. "Okay, Irving. Go up to the front desk and they'll help you with your medication. Please, refrain from rolling around in random mud holes in the future?"

"Snow is coming," I told Helena, and I took a look at the patient charts.

"It is winter," she said. "So, Pell? What will you be doing this year?"

. . .

"I'll be working, I imagine."

"Even during the Food Gathering?"

Winter had always been my favorite season, back when I lived with my parents. It was the season of the Food Gathering, the traditional bear holiday where clans would gather to share a gigantic, hearty meal in symbolic preparation for the winter.

"Too busy," I said. And I was—winter was the time of the Fighting Art's School trials, the time when people tended to get injured falling on some patch of ice or caught a sickness. I hardly had time to spare with the rounds I had to make.

"Hm," she said. "You didn't go home last year, or the year before. Isn't the festival an important time for bear shifters? The time to be with family, or snuggle up with a sweetie?" She smiled and nudged my arm.

"You know how things get around here during winter."

"You're one of the most talented healers I know, and probably the most hardworking. A given, considering your background—you bears have some of the best healing arts in the world—but Hounds of Hell, you need to take a break sometime, Pell. Everyone needs to take some time to look around once in a while. Otherwise, you'll find life has passed you by, and you'll be old, tired and single. Like me."

I chuckled. "Thanks for the warning," I said.

Helena went to assist the doctors at the Pinetown clinic, leaving me to finish taking care of the rest of the patients here. It was early evening when I closed the place up and had the last patient out the door, and the setting sun peeked hazily through grey clouds. I shifted into my bear form and set out on the long walk north to my cabin inside the forest. Even though I'd worked here for four years, I still sometimes got the stares from the occasional wolf, surprised to see a bear roaming through town.

The mentioning of the Food Gathering festival had put me in an odd mood. Admittedly, I did miss those old days of gathering around a cozy fire after filling up on a good meal, just sitting around enjoying the company of loved ones. Times had changed, though. I just couldn't imagine facing my parents after what had happened during the last gathering. It felt like such a long time ago, now.

I reached the border of the forest. Turning my bear nose up to the wind, I took in a long breath of crisp, winter air.

Yup, I thought, *a whole lot of snow will be blowing through these parts soon.*

. . .

I would soon find out that snow wasn't the major change that this year's winter would bring to my little part of the forest.

VANDER

"I still don't understand why you can't just have the driver take you into Diamond Dust," Mom said. "Or at the very least, we could purchase you a car. One of those all-terrain, off-road ones. It'll still be an adventure."

"No, Mom," I sighed. "That would defeat the whole purpose of this trip. If I need a ride, I'll hitchhike. But I plan on going the way to Diamond Dust by foot or paws."

It'd been a week since I'd announced my plans to go out on my little journey, a week in which I'd spent every day looking at the map and dreaming of the adventures I might have on my trip. Today was finally the day I'd set my feet on to the open road. I'd made the decision to travel north to a small resort town called Diamond Dust, which lay at the base of the mountains on the northernmost edge of the forest. I'd walk along the main highway that cut through the forest, passing by a little place called Houndsville, and a bear town called Ursidcomb.

"Well, I don't like the idea of you going through a *bear* town," Mom sniffed.

"I'll be fine," I said. "It's not like I'm going to be living with them, or anything. Just passing through."

"Perhaps you might wait until the spring? Maybe you'll change your mind. After all, the Dawn Academy is still accepting applications, I can speak to my connections in the admissions department..."

"No, Mom," I said. "I'm not going to wait. I need to do this."

She sighed and took me by surprise with a stiff hug. Mom was not the kind of woman who gave us hugs. Out of the corner of my eye, I saw Christophe, Loch and Arthur all exchange a glance. They were equally surprised at this unusual display of warmth from our icy alpha mother.

"You're strong and capable, but you're still an omega," she said. "Don't let your guard down. If you ever need help or want to come home, . "Just call. I'll have a car, a helicopter, a boat, anything. I'll get you home immediately."

. . .

"Okay," I said gently.

Dad gave the straps of my pack a test shake, and then nodded with approval. He had a stern look plastered onto his face, but I could tell that he was holding in his emotions. "Go find what you need, Van," he told me gruffly.

I shook Christophe's hand and then gave Arthur a hug. "Feel lucky," he told me. "Mom and Dad would most definitely not have approved if Christophe, Loch or I had wanted to do such a trip. The perks of being an omega. Make the most of it, yeah?"

Loch and Ian were last. I'd hoped to see Tresten too, but he had class at the FAS.

"Say goodbye to Uncle Van," Loch said to Ian, who'd taken a break from running endlessly around in his pup form. He'd kept his tail shifted out, and it drooped sadly behind him.

"Don't go, Uncle Van," he wailed, clinging onto my leg. "Don't die."

"I'm not going to die," I laughed, petting his head. "I'll just be gone for a couple weeks."

. . .

He sniffled, and went back to his father's side.

"Hey," Loch said, punching my shoulder. "I'm proud of you, Van. If it were me, I would've probably resigned to studying something shitty that I hated. So, good on you for not settling."

"Language," Mom hissed.

"Thanks, bro," I said, pulling him into a tight hug. I was starting to feel weepy and emotional, which meant it was time for me get going before I changed my mind.

"Look out for bears," Loch said, with a lopsided grin.

I set out down the long driveway leading away from the Luna mansion, and took one more look back at my family. *Come on, Van*, I thought. *You crawled through mud, scaled boulders and rock faces, and swam through a lightning storm. Leaving home for a couple weeks should be easy.*

Surprisingly, it was the hardest thing I'd ever done.

* * *

I decided to hitch a ride to the edge of the city, so that I could start the three-day trek through the forest rather than wasting my time walking the never-ending streets of Wolfheart. As I stepped onto the highway leading out north, I stopped for a moment beneath a sign that read "Now Leaving Wolfheart" and looked back for the first time since I'd set out down the driveway. I was at a higher elevation than the city, so it stretched out as a carpet of buildings set into the earth. I could just make out the ancient stonework buildings of the Dawn Academy standing out in the center.

Let's do this, I thought, and turned back to the road. In the far distance ahead of me, I saw white capped mountains that were painted with a shoreline of evergreen forest. That mountain was my destination.

I stopped at a small roadside gas station after walking for a few hours to buy myself a lunch and drink something hot. The further I walked, the colder the air seemed to get.

"Where ye off t'?" the clerk, a grizzled old alpha wolf with salt and pepper hair asked me.

"Diamond Dust," I said, sipping on the tea I bought and munching a sandwich.

"Diamond Dust," he repeated. "Yer on foot?"

"Yes, sir," I replied politely.

. . .

"Hrm. Long way t' Diamond Dust on foot."

"Three days," I said, nodding.

"I kin give yer ride up t' Ursidcomb. If ye dun mind kavootin' with t' bears." He broke into a raspy laugh.

"I appreciate the offer," I replied, "but I need to do this thing on foot. I already got a ride this far."

"I see. Road's hard, not a place fer a young omega like yerself. But what does'n ancient old hound like me know? Suit yerself. Keep'n up this road, 'n ye pass through Houndsville. Y'find some ancient walking routes cuttin' through the forest, too, see, but I dun advise y' use those. Not clearly marked."

"Thank you," I said. After finishing my lunch and my tea, I got back onto the road. The old clerk stood out in front of the station and gave me a wave goodbye.

"How exciting," I said to myself. I'd never been this far outside of the city before, and already everything, including the people, seemed so different.

The idea of an ancient shortcut going through the forest to Diamond Dust intrigued me and caught my imagination. I wondered about what kind of shifters would've used those routes—I knew from my history classes in school that the original packs that had founded Wolfheart had migrated from the far, far icy north, crossing through frozen tundra and cutting through the mountains that Diamond Dust lay at the foot of. Maybe they had used some of those old paths, all those years ago.

Maybe I'll check them out. After all, this was an adventure. What was an adventure without getting off the beaten path? I *could* take the highway all the way through to Diamond Dust, or I could navigate one of those old walking routes. I figured that I could follow one through to Ursidcomb, at least, just to say that I'd done it. I decided that once I arrived in Houndsville, the town at the edge of the forest, I'd investigate into the mystery of the ancient pathway through the forest.

The wind was starting to blow colder and the sky was filled with grey clouds, but I felt free. I was on an adventure.

I made it into Houndsville just after sundown. The town was tiny—way smaller than I had been expecting—though I supposed that everything would seem tiny when the only place I'd ever lived was the city. The highway was the town's main road, which ran down its center and was lined with only a few desolate businesses—a general store, a café that looked like it might've gone out of business years ago, a grungy bar, a healer's clinic, and a small motel called "The Dog's Bark". A single dirt road veered off from the highway, leading out towards the forest and into rows of trailer homes.

. . .

"Might not be another warm motel until I get to Ursidcomb," I said to myself. "Might as well indulge while I'm here."

The Dog's Bark was operated by an old woman with the thickest pair of glasses I'd ever seen, which magnified her golden eyes to an almost comical size. She also had her wolf ears permanently shifted out, and they poked up through her curly white hair.

"I'm just about deaf without them," she explained.

The room was tiny and seemed like it hadn't been redecorated in decades. The wallpaper was peeling off at the tops, the curtains were moth-eaten, and the faucet in the bathtub ran a muddy brown before finally going clear. Above the single bed was a framed painting of a wolf attacking a grizzly bear.

"Huh. That seems awfully old fashioned," I said, observing the controversial painting.

After a quick shower in water that was at first icy cold, and then blistering hot, I slipped into the dusty bed. It'd been a long day, and I was exhausted. I felt myself quickly drifting off to sleep, and the last thing that passed through my mind was the realization of how incredibly *quiet* it was here.

. . .

The next morning when I went downstairs to check out of my room, I found the old lady dozing at the front desk. She woke up when I cleared my throat, and when she opened her eyes, I found myself get startled by the sudden appearance of her gigantic magnified eyes.

"I was wondering," I said, unfolding my map onto the counter, "if you knew anything about the old paths going through the forest towards Diamond Dust."

"Moldy bath?" she asked, giving me a confused look. "Whatcha say? I cleaned the bath tubs myself, just last week…"

"Old paths," I repeated, louder. "I was told there's an ancient, historical walking route that goes through the forest into Diamond Dust." I tapped the location of the mountain town on my map, and the old lady adjusted her glasses and leaned in to look.

"Oh, you mean the forest roads," she said. "I used to walk them when I was half your age. They passed through this way, if I recall." She drew a line with her finger on the map from Houndsville into the forest to Ursidcomb. "—I was never allowed to go that far. Went only to hunt rabbits with my brothers. That was just as far as… around here." She circled a small area by the edge of the forest.

. . .

"It is a road?" I asked. "A clear road?"

"Yes," she said. "Before the highway was here, that's how folks used to get into the mountains. But that was years ago. The highway's been here since the time of my grandpap."

"But I'd still be able to find the path today?"

"I reckon you could," she said, looking at me with her owl-sized eyes. Her ear twitched, and she scratched it. "The entrance is located around here." She pointed to the map. "I don't think they've been maintained, though. Probably better you take the highway if you plan on walking all the way to Diamond Dust. Especially in this cold. And if you ask me, I don't think it's very safe to walk around these parts alone as an omega."

"Thanks for the information," I said.

I walked back up the road until I came to the dirt side-road leading towards the trailer homes scattered on the edge of the forest. According to what the old lady had showed me, the entrance to the old forest roads were in that area. Making my way through the smattering of old and ramshackle homes, I watched as two kids who in their pup forms wrestled in the mud.

. . .

It struck me how poor this place was. My family, despite recent financial problems, had always been wealthy. We were leaders of the Crescent Moon Pack, one of the oldest and strongest wolf clans in the country. I'd spent my entire life waited on, served, and given my every need. Being out here, experiencing how things were outside of my world, was eye-opening. I wasn't completely naïve—I of course knew that I would encounter people of a different class than I was—but it was still a surprise to see it.

Asides from the two playing kids, the neighborhood almost felt like a ghost town. I was glad that I'd chosen to stay in the motel, because I probably wouldn't have felt safe finding a place to camp around here.

I passed by a man with shifty red eyes, sitting out on the steps of a rusty, overgrown trailer. He wore nothing but a pair of stained underwear, and was guzzling from a bottle of alcohol as he puffed on an acrid smelling cigarette. I nodded to him as I passed, and he stared on at me with a strange look in his eye that made me feel uncomfortable. After I'd walked some distance away, I looked back over my shoulder to see if he was still there. He was—only he'd shifted now into his wolf form, his red eyes peeking out from behind matted black fur. The cigarette lay smoldering on the dirt. He licked his chops as he continued to stare after me. I shivered and hurried on.

I really am encountering all sorts of interesting people, I thought to myself.

. . .

A waist-high wall of piled up stones ran along the edge of the forest, and looking at my map I walked alongside it until I reached the place where the entrance to the forest roads was supposed to be located. I climbed over the wall, and shivered as a brisk wind blew at my back. It was getting colder. I set my pack down, removed my shoes and attached them to the outside of my pack. Then I removed my clothing down to my shift-wear, folded them, and put them away. I slid the pack onto my back, adjusted the straps to fit me in my wolf form, and then shifted. Immediately I felt warmer—my winter coat was perfect insulation from this biting wind. And with my senses heightened, I'd be able to locate the entrance to the forest roads without a problem.

I made my way up to the trees and started to sniff around. It wasn't long before I located a stone marker with a worn paw print etched into it. The ground, I could see, was a different color than the surrounding area.

Here it is, I thought, and entered.

* * *

The forest was thick, and the shade of the trees cut the already dim-sunlight down to shadows. I plodded along, sniffing at the ground to keep wind of the trail, which definitely hadn' not been used or maintained in a really long time.

It was my first time in a forest like this. I'd been to the Wolfheart central park, which had a botanical garden and an apple orchard, but never a real, *wild* forest before. Even though there was a kind of comfort in the place that made my wolf form feel at home, I was so not used to everything about it. The quiet, the smells and the darkness all made me feel uneasy.

I'd walked for about an hour when I thought I caught a strange smell carried in on the wind from behind me.

I froze and sniffed at the air. It was gone now, but I could've sworn I'd smelled cigarette smoke. Thinking of that creepy wolf I'd passed in the trailer park, I swallowed nervously, quickening my pace. I found myself straining all my senses, trying to hear or smell if I was being followed. My imagination, which had been fantasizing about the ancient wolves who'd used this path before, now was going wild with other things—namely a creepy, stalker alpha wanting to take advantage of a young omega out in the middle of the woods.

I thought I heard a rustle of branches from somewhere off in the distance, and I froze, my ears perked up high.

"Dammit, Van," I muttered to myself. "It was probably a rabbit or something. What kind of wolf am I? Scared of rabbits…"

That's right, I thought. *What am I worried about? I trained to get into the FAS. I could easy take anyone on who gave me trouble.*

. . .

Right?

I quickened my pace until I was at a brisk trot, my tongue lolling out of my muzzle as I dealt with the encumbering weight of my pack.

You're a fighter, remember? Stop being such a coward.

I tried repeating my clan's words in my mind: *"The wolf of honor, strength and pride treads beneath the Crescent Moon."* It didn't really help. My imagination was raging to the point where my own footfalls were freaking me out.

Suddenly, there was a loud crack of branches from behind me. I didn't even turn to look—I yelped in shock and bolted ahead as fast as I could. In my mind, I saw the black wolf chasing me, his hungry red eyes bearing down on me.

Go! Don't stop!

I kept running, not even certain if anything or anyone was actually following me. At that point, it didn't even matter.

Then, my pack snagged onto a low hanging branch, sending me careening off my feet. Everything twisted and whirled around me as I fell. I felt my pack pull free from my body as I spun. *I fell off a cliff*, I thought, rather calmly. It was the last thing that passed through my mind before everything went black.

PELL

~~~

On the rare days I had off from making my rounds between the three towns, I enjoyed taking long walks around the forest surrounding my cabin. I'd grown up around these woods, but even after spending nearly twenty-seven years here I still found myself in wonder of them.

My nose had been right, of course. A light dusting of snow in the morning turned heavy by the afternoon. By late afternoon, a gorgeous, glittering blanket of clean, white snow covered the forest. I shifted into my bear form and went out to explore the virgin landscape, and to search for a wild boar I could catch and cook for dinner that night.

When I was young, my father used to bring me out into the woods to show me how to hunt boar, catch fish, and forage for berries, both in human and bear forms. Aside from tracking animals and sniffing out berries, things were much more difficult to do in bear form, which was why my father insisted I not rely on tools and do everything the "old-fashioned way" as much as possible. I quickly found that I enjoyed doing things the more challenging way. I think that was why, after completing my studies of bear healing techniques with my father, I'd decided to go into the city. It was a new, and more challenging environment. I wanted to see how my techniques stacked up against those of the big wolf world.

Turned out, we bears really did have some of the best healing knowledge around.

My paws crunched softly through the powder snow, and I stopped to watch a frightened rabbit scamper across my path and into the bushes. A light snowfall continued to drift down, and the forest was whisper quiet. That was one of my favorite parts about the snow, especially after spending time in Wolfheart. I loved how quiet it could get.

I shambled down to a stream and drank my fill of its refreshing, ice-cold water. There were a few trout swimming around, but the ones I saw were small and not ready for eating yet. I continued on through the forest, keeping my eyes, ears and nose peeled for any signs of wild boar.

Eventually I did come across a set of tracks meandering through the snow, but they weren't from a boar—they were from a wolf. I followed them, wondering who would've come through this part of the woods. There were hunters here sometimes, but these tracks didn't seem like they came from a hunter. They were all over the place, with no effort to hide them. I then wondered if maybe it was just someone who'd come exploring from Houndsville, but that also seemed unlikely. I was pretty far out from the town.

When I found some drops of blood on the snow, I became concerned. I hurried my pace. Whoever it was, I quickly realized that they were probably lost. The tracks crisscrossed all over in no certain direction, like they were trying to find their way. I kept walking, and soon I got the scent of a wolf nearby. Then I saw him.

He was sprawled out in the snow, his white fur making him almost invisible except for the patch of red blood on his back. I hurried up to him. He was unconscious, his breathing shallow. He wasn't anyone I recognized from town—I didn't think there were any omegas in Houndsville.

"Better get you back home," I said. The omega stirred at the sound of my voice, and his eyes slowly opened. They were a brilliant blue, and they searched mine before closing again.

"Don't… touch me," he murmured deliriously. "I'll fight you."

"I'd like to see you try," I said, carefully pushing my head beneath him to slide him across my back.

* * *

Back in my human form at my cabin, I wrapped up my still unconscious, still wolf-shifted guest up in blankets and put him next to the fireplace. After getting a fire going, I inspected his wounds, which weren't serious. It seemed like he'd taken a fall somewhere and hit his head, and he had some minor cuts on his back and shoulder. It was lucky that he'd been in his wolf form when he'd had his accident—it seemed as though his fur had protected him from the elements. I wasn't sure how long he'd been out there for. I went through my healing supplies and hooked up him to a special pack of extra hydrating fluids that I'd concocted myself—special bear medicine.

"I'll be right back," I said, and went to go finish searching for a wild boar.

It didn't take me long to find one. I killed it and brought it back to the cabin where I butchered it out in the back and set to making a boar stew. I'd originally wanted to make steaks, but with my unexpected guest I figured something more warming would be better.

He continued to sleep soundly. I got the food on the stove and started to simmer it, and then went to check on him. He wasn't bleeding, and seemed to be in good shape. It'd just depend now on how he was when he came to. Would he remember what happened? How hard had he hit his head?

I sat down in a chair next to him. Though I hadn't seen him in human form, I had to admit that he was... attractive. For a wolf. He was probably around twenty, with white fur and the lean, toned body of an omega.

I could hear my mother's voice in my head, dismayed that I could find a wolf omega attractive. "They're too skinny!" she'd probably say. "Too small. Get a nice, bear omega. What's wrong with a bear omega?"

I sighed.

The wolf stirred, his blue eyes opening a crack. "No," he groaned. "Get away."

"You're safe here," I said. "Don't worry."

"Don't chase." He closed his eyes again and was out.

"Hey," I said, but he didn't respond. I shrugged and went over to check on the food. It was starting to get nice and aromatic. Once the stew was ready, I'd get out the smelling salts to wake him.

There was something familiar about him, I realized. He was definitely not any wolf I'd seen in town, but I thought that I recognized him. Something about those blue eyes of his…

. . .

I tasted the stew, and added some more herbs and spices into the mix. I'd learned to cook from my mother, who'd always prepared the best dishes for the Food Gathering festival. Everyone in the clan agreed that hers were the absolute best. The boar stew I was making was one of her recipes, and although I'd gotten pretty damn good at making it myself, I never managed to top how Mom had done it.

I smiled, remembering the days before the Gathering, when I'd watch her bustle around the kitchen making all her special dishes. She'd sometimes shift out her bear nose to get a stronger whiff of the mixture, and it always used to make me laugh.

"Almost ready," I said to myself, giving the food another quick taste. Not bad, but again, not Mom's.

"Serving my recipe to a wolf!" I could hear her complain. "This was meant for bears, not wolves. You're spending too much time with wolves. Come back home. Be where you belong, with the bears. The bears, Pell."

"Ugh..." My guest was awake again. I looked over my shoulder and was surprised to see that he'd shifted back to human form. He was sitting up, wrapped in the blanket with his back turned to me.

"Hi," I said. "Don't worry, you're safe. Just in time for dinner." I took out two bowls and poured out some stew. He shifted around to look at me. His skin was dotted with sweat, and I could see the ripples of his chest muscles in the shadows beneath the blanket, which was draped over his head like a hood. He reached up and pulled it back, fully revealing his face. Suddenly, I realized who he was, and it seemed like he recognized me too.

"What are you doing here?" we both asked each other at the same time. He blinked, looking confused.

"You're that rescue healer," he murmured. "Am I dreaming? I'm dreaming. I never thought I'd dream about an alpha *bear*, but I guess I'll take it…"

He looked like he was going to pass out again. I set the bowls down and supported him up. He looked at me with dazed eyes.

"You are pretty good-looking," he said absently, with a goofy smile.

"You're not dreaming," I said. "You hit your head, but seeing as though you remember who I am, I guess you don't have any damage up there. What were you doing wandering around my woods?"

I remembered the business card I'd given him the night of the FAS trials, and my offer for him to find me if he decided he'd want to use his skills to save lives—but that card only had my business information on it. There was an address on the back, but that was to the downtown office of HeliHound, the rescue team I worked for. There was nothing about the clinics, nor the location of my home.

He shook his head. "I don't know. Your woods?" He looked confused and spaced out.

"Maybe you do need some time for things to clear up," I said. "Here, eat."

I handed the bowl of stew to him. He tested it, then scarfed it down with wide eyes. "That was delicious," he said.

"There's plenty more," I said. "Let me refill your bowl."

I did, and then sat down in a chair next to fire to eat. "What's your name?" I asked.

"Vander. Vander Luna. So, um…" He paused, waiting for my name.

"Pell Darkclaw."

"Pell, this isn't a dream?"

. . .

"No, you're really here, in my cabin. Do you remember what happened?"

He nodded slowly. "I was… taking the old forest road. Trying to get to… to Diamond Dust."

"Why were you doing that?" I asked, frowning. "The highway takes you straight there."

"I'm on a kind of adventure," he said. "I wanted the challenge."

"I see."

"I was walking through the town, and I went into the forest. And… I think someone—a wolf from the town, an alpha—started to follow me. He chased me, and I fell."

I raised an eyebrow. "An alpha from town chased you in the woods?"

"Well, I think so. I don't know. I never actually saw him."

"Then what makes you think he chased you?"

. . .

His blue eyes turned down to his bowl, and his cheeks turned red. "I heard a noise, and it spooked me."

I did my best to hold back a laugh. "Spooked you? You didn't smell him coming, or anything like that?"

"I smelled cigarettes. He'd been smoking," he said, looking defiant. The look quickly deflated. "But I can't be sure of that either."

I knelt down next to him. "Let me see your arm," I said, and he held out his arm to me. "I'm going to take this out now." I withdrew the IV from him, and moved the stand that had the hydration pack hanging from it. "Well, I'm not going to say it didn't happen. But I've been through Houndsville for a few years now and know most of the people there. I'd say that most likely you imagined it."

"Well, *something* came after me in the forest."

"Most likely," I said, stirring my stew, "the thing that would've come after you is in this stew right now. Wild boar. They can be incredibly aggressive. One's even taken a charge at me, even in my bear form."

. . .

Vander stared at his bowl, silently contemplating what I'd said. It was obvious from the expression on his face that he was extremely embarrassed. Honestly, it was kind of cute.

"So, this is the second time I've rescued you, huh?"

"Hey, I didn't need rescuing that first time," he huffed. "I was fine."

"Right." I nodded and slurped down the rest of the stew. "You went after that guy. That was really something. So, they never ended up offering you honorary entrance to the school or anything, huh?" I held out my hand to him. "More stew?"

He shook his head no, and I took his bowl to go wash up. "The FAS doesn't work that way."

"You'd think they give commendation for bravery," I said, and put the kettle on the stove to boil some water for tea.

"They reward entrance to only the most dedicated," he said flatly. "Even if it means watching the man next to you drown."

"And that is something I'll never understand."

. . .

The kettle whistled and I made two mugs of tea.

"Thank you," he said, taking the mug from me. "For rescuing me out there. I remember when I came to, I was covered in snow. It was so cold. I walked around for hours, trying to find the path, but it was hidden underneath the snow. I couldn't smell anything. I... would've died if you hadn't come along."

I nodded. "It's a good thing I was there."

He looked at me, the soft light of the fire flickering against his cheek. "I never thought I'd ever owe my life to a *bear*."

I walked to the window and looked outside. It was mostly dark, but I could still see the snow coming down in billowing white sheets. "And I never thought I'd be stuck with an omega wolf," I said with a resigned smile. "I'm sorry to tell you this, Vander, but your adventure is going to be put on hold. Until this weather clears, neither of us will be going very far from this cabin."

VANDER

It was difficult for me to sleep that night. My whole body ached, especially my right leg, which was throbbing with pain. Pell mixed up a bitter concoction and told me it was special "bear medicine."

"We bears have the best healing techniques," he told me, seeing my hesitant look. "Surely you know that?"

I shook my head. The only thing I knew about bears was that they mostly liked to live out in the woods and other rural areas, and according to popular wolf opinion, they were lazy, dumb, and could be untrustworthy. I knew that was an outdated way of thinking, but I didn't really know any bears in real life and so it still hung in the back of my mind—though Pell didn't seem to fit the stereotype at all. He had a kind face and intelligent eyes, and didn't seem to be the least bit lazy, dumb or untrustworthy. Still, I wasn't used to bears.

. . .

I definitely wasn't used to his *size*. He was so big. He stood over six and half feet tall at least, and his stocky, thickly muscled build was much larger than most wolf alphas. For his aggressive stature, Pell had a surprisingly gentle demeanor and grace about the way he moved and did things. I kept it to myself, but I thought it was pretty funny how small certain things looked compared to him—the kettle, and other various items he had in his cabin that'd obviously been designed for the average wolf hands and not a bear shifter's.

I drank down the rest of the bear tonic, and not too long afterwards the pain eased. Still, I squirmed beneath my blanket set out on a pile of soft furs on the floor, unable to get comfortable and sleep. The fire was low, throwing dim orange light around the tiny cabin. I turned over to look at Pell's bed. He was curled up under his blanket, like a breathing mountain.

Slipping out from under my blanket, I went over to the window. The snow was coming down hard, glittering in the light of the moon. I sighed, feeling stupid. If it hadn't been for my luck, I might've died. And even if I hadn't taken the forest roads, I could've gotten caught in this snow storm before reaching Ursidcomb. I'd gotten overconfident and royally screwed up planning my little "adventure."

I glanced over my shoulder at Pell. *Or maybe I was getting the adventure I'd wanted?* I was okay, just a little bruised up with a wounded ego, but I was safe. I went back to my nest of furs and blankets, curled up and drifted into sleep.

. . .

That night, I dreamed Mom and Dad flew in a helicopter to bring me home. Tendril-like ropes descended down from the chopper, wrapping around my body and yanking me from the forest. "No!" I protested. "I can still go." I fought against the ropes but couldn't get myself free, and as I was hoisted up towards the roaring helicopter, I saw my parents looking disappointedly down at me.

"We knew you couldn't do it," Mom said.

I felt a hand grab at me, and looked down to see Pell grabbing at me, trying to free me and pull me down.

"We knew you'd fail," said Dad. "You're weak, that's why. Nobody would want someone so weak."

"You'll be safe at home," agreed Mom. "Just come home."

"Vander," Pell said. "Fight. You can do it. Fight. Vander. Vander."

I opened my eyes to Pell looking down at me, his eyes concerned. "Vander," he said gently.

"Huh?" I shivered. I was cold, and covered in sweat. My body ached.

. . .

"Hi," Pell said, dabbing a warm, damp towel to my forehead. "You were having a nightmare, I think. Relax. You have a fever."

I looked around, confused. "Am I sick?"

"I think I missed something yesterday when I was checking your wounds. Something must've gotten hidden by your fur, and I didn't see it. It might be infected. You're going to have to do me a favor."

"Huh," I groaned. I was completely out of it. My head throbbed, and I could feel my body trembling. I pulled the blankets up tighter in an effort to get warm. "What?"

"I need to take your clothes off."

I blinked and cinched up the blankets even tighter. "What?"

"I'm sorry," he said. "But I think you may have something inside you—a splinter, or something. I just need to examine you to make sure."

"I c-can examine myself," I said stubbornly, shivering. Pell wiped the sweat from my head. I felt worse than I had yesterday.

. . .

Pell sighed. "Okay, suit yourself. I guess you can handle removing whatever you might find, too?" He stood up and drew open the curtains, but only small slants of light filtered in. The window was mostly dark, and I realized why—it was completely covered up with snow. I watched with weary, aching eyes as Pell turned on the rest of the lights in the cabin. He went to a cabinet, pulled out a tiny mirror, and placed it next to me. "I'm going to dig the snow away from the door. You can use the bathroom to check yourself."

"What's t-this for?" I asked, referring to the mirror.

"How else are you going to look at your own back?" he said, and pulled a shovel out from a cabinet by the front door.

Groaning, I pushed the covers off of me. My clothes were soaked. I was so hot, but freezing cold at the same time. I picked up the mirror and then slinked off to the bathroom.

After stripping down and undoing the bandages that Pell had dressed me in, I did my best to contort my body to try and get a look at my back in the reflection of the tiny handheld mirror being reflected off the just as tiny mirror on the bathroom wall. I could hear the chuff of snow as Pell shoveled away at the front door.

The mirror on the wall was so small and hung in such an inconvenient place that I literally couldn't see anything but my shoulders. Finally, I poked my head out of the bathroom.

What I saw nearly made me drop the mirror in surprise. Pell had set the shovel aside and was in his bear form, using his huge claws to dig out the snow that'd piled up in front of the door. He'd broken through the top half, and I could see snow was still blowing down.

"Pell," I said in a weak voice.

He turned around, and I flinched back slightly. He was tall in his human form already, but in his bear form he was *towering*.

"Yeah?" He asked, his voice booming.

"I... can you look?"

At that, he shifted back to his human form. In nothing but his shifter wear, the tight fitting underwear that allowed him to shift without screwing up his clothes, I got a full view of his bulging and rippling muscles. I felt a strange feeling inside, and I wasn't sure if it was the fever or something else. He quickly pulled a robe from the wall and wrapped himself up with it.

"Yes, I can," he said. "If you can agree to trust me and do what I ask."

. . .

I nodded, feeling too embarrassed and too exhausted to protest.

"Yeah, okay," I said. "Just don't do anything weird."

"I'm a doctor," he said, his voice even. "This is my job."

I nodded, feeling a little more comfortable. Pell picked up one of the blankets from the ground. "You can wrap this around your front."

I took it from him and then came out from the bathroom. I faced my bare back to him, holding the blanket so that it hung down the front of my body. He kneeled down behind me, and my imagination started to race. *Where was he looking?*

"I'm going to touch your right thigh," he said, and I nodded. Despite the warning, I still felt a little shiver run through me as his fingers made contact with my flesh. I had a wound that ran up from the back of my thigh up to my lower back from when I fell down the hill, and his fingertips probed the area. I thought I felt his breath on my skin, but I couldn't be sure if it was just my overactive, fever-driven imagination.

"Ahh, ow."

"Does it hurt here?"

. . .

"Well, yeah, I'm kind of fucked up right there and you're poking around it."

Pell said nothing, continuing check me.

"Sorry," I mumbled. "I'll be quiet."

His fingers followed the wound up my thigh. "It's swollen and hot," he said. "There's definitely... ah. Right here. Open your legs a bit, please."

My face was getting hotter, and it wasn't because of the fever. I took a slight step to the right with one foot. I couldn't see it, but I could feel him leaning closer to inspect me. I could sense the proximity of his face to the inside of my exposed thigh, and it was getting me weirdly excited.

What the hell is wrong with me? Why is this turning me on? Am I that fucking delirious right now?

"There's a splinter, or a piece of something stuck in the wound." I heard the clacking of metal as he rooted through his equipment bag. "Okay, hold still. I'm going to extract it."

. . .

I gritted my teeth as a sudden sharp pain shot through my leg, and then was gone.

"Here it is," Pell said, standing up. I turned around and Pell held up a tiny, needle-like splinter with a pair of steel tweezers. He tossed it in the trash. "The wound is still infected. I don't have the proper ingredients to make medicine for it here, and with the snow how it is we can't get into Houndsville."

"What will I do?" I asked.

Pell handed me a glass of water. "First off, you need to drink. I have a highly effective treatment, but it'll sound unusual to a wolf like yourself."

"Why?"

"It's a traditional bear healing method."

"That's fine, you gave me that bear tonic last night and it worked. It tasted terrible, but I can deal with it."

"This isn't a tonic," he said, seriously.

"What is it, then?"

. . .

"Bear shifter saliva," he said.

I made a face. "I have to drink spit?"

"No... It needs to be a direct application."

I stared at him. "I told you nothing weird, and you want to do something weird."

"It's not something I would do for my normal patients, for obvious reasons. Wolves don't know about it. But ask any bear, and they'll tell you it works."

"I don't see any other bears around that I can ask," I said. "I'm really grateful to you for saving my ass out there, but I don't feel so great about you *licking* it too."

"Right back at you," he said coolly. "You think I want to? But there isn't any other choice."

I felt dizzy and sat down on my bed of furs. Pell refilled my water. "Drink. You need to drink more."

"Maybe I can just ride it out," I said.

. . .

He shook his head. "I don't think you want to risk it. If you could see what it looked like, you would agree with me."

"Bear saliva," I said shaking my head. "You just want to do something weird to me."

He sighed. "Trust me, it's the last thing I want to do."

My leg was throbbing with pain and heat. It definitely did not feel like it was in very good condition at all. I didn't have much choice.

"Okay, fine. Do it. Just make it quick."

"Stand up," he said. "Or lie on your stomach, if you feel you can't stand."

I unwrapped the blanket, exposing my back, and lay on my stomach.

"I'm going to shift now," he said. "Keep still, so I don't have to do this for any longer than I have to."

. . .

He dropped his robe to the ground, and I watched as Pell's muscles expanded and morphed. His bones popped and crunched as they rearranged and changed shape, and thick brown fur erupted from his skin. His ears became round and moved to the top of his head, and his face pushed out, becoming a bear muzzle. The shift completed, Pell walked behind me, the floor of the cabin trembling with his movements.

"Ready?" he asked.

"Just do it," I said.

"It might tickle a bit..."

I squeezed my eyes shut, trying to prepare myself. When I felt Pell's bear tongue make contact with my leg, I nearly screamed in shock. Nothing could've prepared me for how it felt. It was hot, even against the warmth of the wound, and felt like a melting stick of butter. As his tongue traveled up the back of my thigh, a massive shiver jolted through my body. It actually felt... *good*. *Really good*. It was hot at first, but I felt a tingling sensation spread through the area he'd licked. He continued up, rolling across my right cheek to my lower back, the entire area prickling with numbness.

"Okay," he said.

. . .

I let out a quiet sigh. *I'm disappointed it's over. Why am I disappointed it's over?* I looked over my shoulder and saw Pell was already back in human form. He went over to the sink and rinsed out his mouth. I put my head down onto the furs and closed my eyes.

"Get some rest now," Pell said, pulling the blanket over me. "I'm going to make lunch. I hope you're not tired of boar."

"Thanks," I said quietly. "Thanks for helping me, Pell."

The wound continued to tingle, and it already seemed to feel less swollen, less hot. I was glad that I didn't have to stand up again. I didn't think there would be a way for me to hide the excitement that was now very apparent on my front side.

That was weird, I thought. *So weird. But I liked it.* I cracked one eye open and watched Pell working away at the stove, his robe hanging loosely over his muscles.

I liked it, was the last thought I had before falling asleep.

PELL

The e-mail I'd been writing to Dr. Elpaw sat unfinished on my laptop, the cursor blinking in wait. I stared blankly at the screen. My mind was elsewhere.

"How long was I asleep?" came a groggy voice from behind me.

I turned and saw Vander sitting up. "About two hours. How do you feel?"

"Better," he said. "A lot better."

I could tell right away by just looking at him—his eyes were clear and lucid. He wasn't flushed.

. . .

"My leg isn't throbbing like hell anymore."

"Mmhm," I said.

"I'm sorry," Vander said, looking embarrassed. "I shouldn't have doubted you."

"Don't worry about it," I said. "I understand. It's a pretty unorthodox method for someone unfamiliar with it." I went to the dresser and offered a set of clean clothes to Vander. He'd been wearing a simple robe, since when I'd rescued him in the snow he was in his naked wolf form and had lost his pack in the tumble.

He took them from me, still looking bashful. I found it surprisingly cute.

"You're too generous," he said. "How can I repay you for helping me?"

I shook my head. "This is what I do. It's my life. I don't expect anything back from you."

"So, I'm not the first wolf you've pulled in from the mountain and licked back to health?" He cracked a smile, and I couldn't help but laugh.

. . .

"No, you're the first. I don't often get stuck in the woods with a patient. You must be hungry?"

"Starving," he said, and I averted my eyes as he started to get dressed. Vander was an omega, and his slender build reflected that. Despite his smaller size, he had this excited, almost nervous energy about him. I remembered when I first met him at the FAS trials. When I'd pulled him out of the water after he'd saved the guy who was drowning, Vander had asked me to let him go back in. That was what I was talking about—he seemed like the kind of person who could never take "no" for an answer. He was stubborn, and I liked that. I'd treated hundreds of patients through the clinics and rescued dozens as a part of HeliHound, but never had felt anything more than the usual obligation a healer has to those under his care, and occasionally, some familiarity with those who I'd routinely cared for. But with this omega wolf, who'd stumbled into my life twice now…

I would've given any patient the traditional bear healing treatment if they absolutely needed it. That was my oath as a healer. It was a simple act which I'd done before for patients back home in Ursidcomb, but with Vander it felt different… *really* different. For one, the buzzy, flustered feeling I'd gotten—and did my best to hide—after I performed the treatment on him. What was up with that?

"Lunch is boar chops," I told Vander, getting the food out from the fridge. "Let me heat it up on the stove for you."

. . .

He nodded. "Thank you. Once I'm able to get back on my way, I'd like to give you some cash to pay you back for everything you've done. At the very least, for the food you've given me."

"You don't need to do that," I said.

"I just don't feel right accepting your help for free."

"Not everything is about money. I'm helping you because I want to." I lit the stove, heated up my cast iron skillet, and reheated the boar chop while grilling a few slices of onion on the side. "Tell you what. You want to repay me? Consider what I told you that day at the trials. Look into nurturing that urge you have to help people. The last thing this world needs is another fighter."

Vander's lips tightened, and he said nothing. I pulled the chop off the skillet onto a plate, and continued to grill the onions.

"I didn't think bears used computers," he said. "Do you even get internet out here?"

"Wireless satellite," I replied, pointing at the roof. "And despite what you might've been told, bears aren't backwards bumpkins. Not all of us, at least." I scraped the onions over the chop and brought the plate over to Vander. He dug in, and I sat down across from him and woke up the laptop to continue writing my letter.

"This is really good," he said, his eyes wide and mouth full of boar chop. "Hounds of Hell."

"We bears are good at three things: Healing, cooking and eating."

"I've heard that you have a whole holiday dedicated to eating. Is that true?"

I smiled. "Yeah, you heard right. It's called the Food Gathering festival. It's next month, actually. Everyone gathers up with their family and loved ones, and sometimes the entire clan, and there's a gigantic feast. People compete to see who can cook the best dishes, so you can bet you've never had better eating."

"That sounds amazing," Vander said. "The closest thing we have is the Howling. That's in February. But it's serious and boring. No feast or anything like that."

"I know what the Howling is," I said, chuckling. "I work with wolves, mostly, remember? The Food Gathering festival is something else. It's a very bear tradition, for sure. And my mother, she made the *best* food at the Gathering. It was to die for."

. . .

"Well, you must be excited about it," he said, scarfing down the remainder of the boar chop. "You get to go home and be with your family. Eat good food, get away from work."

"I... haven't celebrated the festival in years," I admitted.

"Why not? Isn't it important?"

"It's a very busy time of the year for me," I said, not wanting to delve too much into the topic.

"As a helicopter rescue healer?" Vander asked.

"When I'm not doing that, I volunteer my time at several healing clinics. I was supposed to do my rounds tomorrow, but with the weather like this, I'm stuck. That's why I'm writing this e-mail, to tell the head doctor that I'm trapped with you."

"Must be hard," he said. "Missing out on a big family celebration like that. You must miss your family and your clan. I hate the Howling, but I still couldn't imagine missing it. Even if my family does annoy the hell out of me sometimes. Hey, since you have a connection here, can I use your computer when you're done? I should let my parents know that I'm okay. I lost everything with my pack."

. . .

"Of course," I said.

It was difficult for me to imagine going back to see my parents after what had happened. The more years I spent away, the easier it became to put our distance in the back of my mind. And anyway, what I'd said about work was the truth.

When I'd finished writing the e-mail to Dr. Elpaw, I turned the computer over to Vander and went to the window. Peeking out of the small gap of space that the snow didn't reach at the top, I could see the outside still shrouded in a white haze of falling snow. I snuck a glance over at Vander.

What was this feeling?

It'd been there as the tiniest little spark from the moment I saw him lying hurt in the snow.

I couldn't really be attracted to a wolf, could I? A wolf omega?

He'll be out of here soon, I reminded myself. *You'll go back to work and you won't see him again. End of story.*

. . .

Besides, I *wasn't* into wolves. No way.

"When do you think that this weather will clear up?" Vander asked. "I'm making my way to Diamond Dust."

"I'd give it another day," I said. "But you're not going to be going to Diamond Dust, not yet. Not on foot. It's way too far and too dangerous. You'll need to go back to Houndsville, wait for the roads to clear, and then catch a ride."

"I'll walk to Ursidcomb first," he said. "It's not too far."

"Ursidcomb is my hometown," I said, "and it's too far. Don't push your luck again…"

"Awesome!" he said, his face lighting up. "If you're from there, you can guide me."

I sighed. "I'll guide you back into Houndsville, but not Ursidcomb."

He gave me an inquiring look. "Why not? It's not that much further."

"Because… it's just not a good idea. And from Ursidcomb you're going to walk to Diamond Dust? I told you, it's dangerous. You'll have better luck catching a ride from Houndsville."

"Why can't I catch one from Ursidcomb?"

He was asking just to be difficult—I could tell he had no plans to catch a ride.

"Because," I said, "it's a small town. There's not many people. And… because it's a bear town. You're not going to find many people volunteering to give a wolf a ride, even if you are an omega."

"Well, if you come with me, then…"

"I'm not going to Ursidcomb," I said loudly.

"Okay, okay," Vander said, shrinking down. I immediately felt bad.

After a couple deep breaths to regain my composure, I got a map from the cabinet and spread it out on the table. "We're here," I said, pointing to a spot inside the vast space marked "Northern Forest." "Diamond Dust is up here, still a two day walk away, and that's without snow. With this weather, it'll be longer. There could be more snowfall, or a freeze. If you're really that set on going up there, then I'll walk you back south, and I'll help you find a ride. Okay?"

"Alright," Vander said, looking resigned. "Sorry. I don't mean to be difficult."

"Why do you want to go to Diamond Dust so badly, anyway?" I asked. "I understand you're traveling, but why there?"

"I wanted to get away from everything. From Diamond Dust I was going to go out camping, just to spent time alone where I could think. I wanted an adventure, and relying on my own two feet or four paws to get there was a big part of it."

That evening, after a dinner of braised boar shanks with grilled spinach and parsnips, I got a fire going and asked Vander if I could inspect his wounds to make sure they were healing okay. After removing his clothes, he covered up his front with the blanket and stood waiting for me to examine him. I felt my heart start to race, and I scolded myself.

Chill out, I thought. *You're a professional.*

The light of the fire rippled over the curves of his shoulders and back, and despite my efforts, my heart still pounded heavily in my chest. He had a gorgeous body.

. . .

You've examined plenty of attractive people before. Get it together, there's nothing different about this.

But there was, and I couldn't explain why.

What was happening to me?

I took a step forward and went down to my knees, fighting the urge to ogle his perfect behind.

Hell, I'd *licked* him there this morning. Why was seeing him getting me all flustered now?

"Well? Does it look okay? I'm not interested in having you stare at my butt for any longer than necessary."

I coughed. "So, tell me," I said, trying to distract myself from what I was feeling. "Does your trip have anything to do with what happened at the FAS trials?"

He was silent for a moment. "Maybe."

"Uh-huh." I gently took his leg and slid it to the side so I could get a look at the inside of his thigh, where the wound made its way up to his behind. I did my best not to let my gaze wander over to anything sensitive, but it was hard.

Professional, I thought. *Professional, professional, professional.*

"There was something my brother-in-law told me that night," Vander continued. "He said that the FAS wasn't the only way. My entire life, I'd thought that the school was the epitome of everything that was great. My father was a graduate. My favorite brother, and my brother-in-law, and all the heroes I'd had as a kid. I wanted to be strong like them and prove that I was special, that I wasn't just some weak omega. Getting into the Fighting Arts School was how I was going to do that. When Kris nearly drowned and no one seemed to care, it made me wonder if it was all as glorious as I had believed it to be."

"And what have you found?"

"I don't know," he said softly. "I'm still looking."

"Everything looks fine," I said, standing up.

"Okay."

I turned around to let him get dressed.

. . .

"So," he said, "I guess once the weather clears up, I'll be out of here."

I felt an awful tightness grip my heart.

Damn, what the hell is wrong with me? I'd never felt this way about anyone—especially a patient. Why did I feel like I didn't want Vander to be out of my life so soon? Why did I wish I had more time to get to know him? What was it about this guy that was so damn attractive to me?

Maybe it was for the best that he was going to be on his way soon. I didn't want whatever I was feeling to progress any further.

"That's right," I told him. "I'll take you back to Houndsville and help you find a ride up to Diamond Dust. You can be back on your adventure."

"And that'll be that?" he asked. Was that sadness I detected in his voice, or was I just projecting? He looked back at me with cool, blue eyes.

"That'll be that," I said.

VANDER

Two days later, the little thrill I'd gotten from Pell's tongue treatment was still floating around in my mind—and my nethers. Part of me wanted to get injured again, just so that I could repeat the experience. The other part of me was impatient about moving on to Diamond Dust, especially because of the way I was feeling about Pell. I had a mission to get on with, and an adventure to complete. I didn't want whatever it was I was feeling to distract me from what I needed to do. I had places to go, people to meet, and *me* to discover. All of that lay ahead in Diamond Dust, not here in the middle of the woods. If anything, the excitement of the past couple days had made me work up even more of a craving for a challenge. I wanted to be tested, and to see what else lay in store on the road ahead.

Pell seemed to be keeping his distance from me—or as much distance as was possible in a tiny cabin. Whenever there was a break in the snowfall, he'd excuse himself to go outside to clear snow from away and to chop wood for the fireplace.

The third time he'd gone out, I began to wonder just how much wood he needed for the damn thing.

My wounds were healing fast, and by the third day most of the pain had gone away. Each night, Pell examined me, and each time I had to fight to kill the racy thoughts that stirred up in my overactive imagination. Normally, standing naked and having anyone, even a healer, look at my body would've made me feel uncomfortable, but with Pell it excited me. Secretly I enjoyed the examinations. I liked knowing his eyes were scanning the places I couldn't see.

"I'm going out," Pell said, pulling on a coat. "Going to chop firewood."

"Sure," I said to the door that was already swinging shut behind him, a little wisp of snow swirling inside.

I sighed and started to pace around the cabin. How much longer until I could get on my way? I was really starting to grow restless, and the tension that seemed to be building between me and my rescuer wasn't helping things.

I spread open the map on the floor and traced the highway up to Diamond Dust with my finger, passing through the small area marked "Ursidcomb." Pell was so against taking me there, and I had the feeling that there was more to it than the town disliking wolves.

. . .

Beside Pell's bed was a small shelf filled with all sorts of old books on the healing arts. I went over to and scanned over the titles. There was one in particular that stood out to me, not because it sounded very interesting, but because the book itself was much older looking than all the rest. Its cover and binding were worn and faded and it looked like the thing might've been older than the both of us combined. I gently pulled it down and read the cover.

"Guide to the Bear Healing Arts, First Volume, First Edition."

There was a handwritten note scrawled onto the first page that read, "May this book help you as much on your journey as it had for me. Signed, your father."

I flipped the page, and something slipped out and fell onto the floor. I picked it up. It was a small photograph of a teenaged Pell standing with a respectful smile next to an older man who I guessed was his father. I could see that Pell was holding the book in his hand.

Pell had told me he hadn't been back home in years. Had something happened? Was that why he didn't want to go back?

I put the photo back between the pages and returned the book to the shelf. After a moment's thought, I dug into Pell's closet for a warm jacket and then went outside into the snow.

. . .

I found Pell sitting on a log by the woodpile, staring off into the trees, his back facing me. I grinned and gathered up a snowball, aimed, and then let it loose. It thwapped onto the back of his head, and he shouted and fell over in surprise.

"Hey!" he shouted, and staggered back to his feet.

"Chopping wood, huh?" I said.

Pell shrugged with a guilty smile, and then scooped up a handful of snow. I yelled and jumped to the side, barely dodging it.

"Is that my jacket?" he shouted, already scooping up another snowball.

"I stole it from your closet. Hope you don't... mind!" I hurled a fist-full of snow at him, and it pelted him right in the chest. His whizzed by me, a far miss, and popped against the side of the cabin.

"You're not very good at this, are you?" I shouted, laughing. Pell grinned back at me, and started to scoop up a gigantic snow boulder. I held up my hands. "Wait! Wait, not fair!" I tried to run, but my feet sunk into the deep, powdery snow.

It smacked me right in the back, sending me face first into the snow.

"You okay?" Pell asked, lifting me up to my feet. He had a cheeky grin on his face, and his cheeks were flushed from the cold. I was taken aback by how attractive I found him at that moment.

"I think you opened one of my wounds," I said, faking a grimace.

His grin vanished immediately. "Shit. I'm sorry. Let's get you back inside, I can check... why are you smiling?"

"You should've seen your face," I said, laughing.

"Oh, you son of a..." He pushed my shoulder and sent me sprawling out onto the snow again. I couldn't stop laughing at the thought of how serious he'd gotten all of a sudden. Pell dove into the snow next to me, covering me in a shower of icy powder. I looked over at him, and he returned the glance, his red eyes flashing brightly. He smiled, and I felt my heart leap. I quickly turned my gaze away to the sky, where snowflakes were swirling down from a carpet of grey-white clouds.

"Pell, why'd you become a healer?" I asked.

. . .

"Just about the same reason you wanted to become a fighter," he said. "I'm from a long line of healers in my family. Our skills are well known in Ursidcomb. My family has a practice back home that's been operating for generations, back to a time when Ursidcomb was just a small village. My father is a healer, my grandfather—all the men I looked up to."

"So, there was never really a question about what you would do," I said.

"I was going to be a healer, whether I wanted to or not. I guess it's fortunate that it'd always been my life's passion. I want to help people, and there are so many who need it."

A cold wind whistled through the trees, and Pell got up from the snow. "It's going to start coming down again, soon," he said. "Help me bring some of this firewood inside."

Pell scooped up two huge armfuls of the wood, carrying them back in like they were nothing. I followed suit with a much smaller, single pile, and followed him back into the cabin just as thick billows of snow started to blow down from the sky.

Soon, Pell had a fire roaring in the fireplace. He filled up the kettle and put it on the stove for tea. After the water boiled, he poured it into two mugs, then got out a big jar of honey, dipped a spoon into it, and stirred the golden stuff into the tea. I watched as he licked the spoon clean, and felt a little shiver of excitement run through my body. I looked away, and told myself to calm down.

"Tea," Pell said, placing the mug in front of me.

"Thanks," I said, and sipped on it. It was more honey than tea, but the flavor was deep and floral and incredibly delicious. "This is really good."

He smiled. "It's honey from Ursidcomb," he said. "You can't find anything like that in Wolfheart, I can promise you that."

A question nagged on my mind. "Pell," I said, "you said that your family has done healing in Ursidcomb for generations. Why aren't you working at your family practice? Why are you out here?"

The smile on his lips faded, and he sipped his tea. For a moment, it seemed like he wasn't going to answer my question.

"Like I told you," he said quietly with a hint of tension in his voice, "I want to help people, and there are a lot of people who need my help. A whole lot more people than in a tiny, isolated bear town where nobody ever wants to leave—or let others in. Our clan has some of the best healing techniques around, Vander. The best. And those skills are being held prisoner there."

. . .

His voice had grown thick with emotion. His reaction took me by surprise, and I realized that I'd touched on a sensitive subject. I thought about the book from his father, and I wondered how this connected with him not going back to visit home for so long, but kept my mouth shut.

Pell must've noticed my stunned expression. He sank down, and the tension immediately disappeared from his face. He sipped on his tea and turned away.

"My mission in life is to help people," he said. "And I can't help people if I'm stuck in a place like Ursidcomb."

My heart was thudding hard in my chest. I was excited by his intensity, and at that moment, I saw Pell a little differently than before. His passion had been bared, and it glowed as brightly as the spirit of any skilled fighter that I knew.

That night, Pell didn't need to ask me if it was alright to do the routine examination. I wordlessly stripped out of my clothes and stood completely in the usual spot by the fireplace, ditching even the usual blanket I used for modesty.

I closed my eyes, waiting for Pell's practiced healer's touch, the precise movements of examination that I knew he'd perfected after doing it hundreds of times. I could feel him behind me, and I hear him lowering down to his knees to bring the wound along my leg and backside up to his eye level. His fingers traced the wound, and even though I told myself I'd gotten used to it, I still shivered.

As he moved up, I had the sudden realization that something felt very different about the way he touched me tonight. It wasn't the usual professional, benign touch from the past times. *Was I just imagining it?* As he made his way up my thigh and to my ass, my pulse started to race as hard as it had during his special tongue treatment.

Pell reached the top of the wound, where the examination would stop and he'd tell me his prognosis. This time, he didn't stop. His fingers moved up my lower back, trailing their way along my spine. I couldn't suppress another shiver.

Was he going to examine my other wounds? I'd been injured along my left shoulder too, but it wasn't nearly as bad as my leg wound and so Pell hadn't bothered checking it as often. I kept my eyes squeezed shut. I felt him move closer to me, his fingers coming up to the base of my neck. I could feel the hairs there raising up in buzzy excitement. His touch moved to my shoulder—my uninjured right shoulder. Then I felt his other hand on my arm. I inhaled a quick and silent gasp as both of his thickly muscled arms moved around my shoulders and pulled me tightly against him. My heart was pounding so hard I thought it might burst.

What is happening?

. . .

That's when I felt Pell's warm lips press against my neck. That time I wasn't able to keep quiet. A surprised moan of excitement escaped from my lips as I tilted my head to expose more to him.

Pell is...

I felt my cock stiffen up immediately as he kissed my neck, occasionally raking my skin with his teeth. I felt the nip of his fangs, and I bit my lip to try to keep myself from letting out any more embarrassing noises.

I want more...

He didn't say a word as his hands moved down from my shoulders to my pecs. His fingertips teased at my firm nipples before continuing their way down to my abs.

"Pell..." My voice was a breathy moan, and I knew it was oozing with want for what was going to come next. I'd never been with anyone before...

His fingers pushed their way through my pubes until they found their target, and my mouth dropped open in a wordless gasp as his massive fist wrapped around my cock. I couldn't have protested, even if I wanted to. It felt too fucking good, and every perfect stroke was sending my body and mind out of control. I couldn't believe what was happening, but at the same time I knew it was exactly what I'd wanted to happen. *How's this for an adventure?*

Pell's free arm was wrapped tightly across my chest, pulling my body against his. My ass ground up against him, and I could feel the swelling hardness of his excitement there. I reached behind me to feel him, and the moment my fingers made contact with his bulge, he groaned with pleasure and squeezed my cock even more tightly. His strokes came faster and harder, working my cock to the point where my legs were becoming quivering pools of jelly. If he hadn't been holding me against him, I probably wouldn't have been able to support my own weight. It felt *amazing*, and each pump of his fist made me more and more helpless. I slipped my hand down the front of his pants, eager to feel him, to have my very first cock.

Hounds of Hell! He was fucking *huge*. His erection filled up my entire fist, and felt just about as thick as my fucking *forearm*. He throbbed mightily in my grasp, as strong and big as I would've expected from a bear alpha. I was so intrigued to know what he looked like. My body and mind had been completely overtaken with an incredible, pulsing desire for my rescuer. I broke free from his grasp and turned around, dropping down to my knees in front of him. Pell looked at me with his gleaming red alpha's eyes, his typically calm expression now marked with a potent and obvious look of dangerous lust. Every muscle in his body seemed to have hardened, and he was absolutely thrumming with an alpha energy I'd never experienced or seen before in my entire life. No wolf alpha could match this.

. . .

I went for the fastener on Pell's pants. He tugged his shirt over his head and threw it aside. I had the fastener undone, and pulled his pants down to his ankles. His erection pushed up the front of his underwear, making it look like it might rip right out from the strain of it. A trail of dark hair crept up from the waistband to his belly button, and I ran my fingers through it before finally yanking his underwear down and letting him pop free.

It was the very first time I'd seen another man's cock, and my eyes widened at the sight of him. A log in the fireplace cracked, sending a dance of sparks up into the chimney, and the orange light gleamed off of his thickly veined tumescence. Its head was dark and shiny, with a delicious drop of precum forming at the tip. I felt my mouth water for him. I took his heat in my hand and ran my nose and lips along its length, starting from the base and slowly moving to the tip. He had a deep and musky smell that stirred excitement down between my legs.

This is *an adventure...*

Pell looked down at me, watching me take my time exploring my very first cock, and he bit his lower lip and let out a low growl.

"I've never done this before," I said, before opening my mouth and taking him inside me. I tasted his flavor on my tongue, and I craved more. I sucked him down, hoping that I knew what I was doing. Pell's head lulled back and he let out a long groan.

"Fuck," he murmured. "That feels amazing."

I smiled and swirled my tongue around his head before swallowing him down deep. *How's that for a tongue treatment?*

I could feel warmth spreading down to my opening as I became wet with excitement—the natural benefit of being an omega. Pell licked his lips, seeming to taste my desire on the air. He pulled his cock from my mouth, a silvery strand of my saliva hanging from its tip to my chin. I didn't need to be told a thing—I turned around and presented myself to him, arching my back and sticking my ass up high.

Pell ran his huge palms across my ass, his touch becoming gentle when they reached the scabs of my injuries. I shivered with anticipation, spreading my legs a little bit.

"This is your first time?" he asked in a low voice as he slipped on a condom.

I nodded, and before he could say anything more, I reached back, grasped his cock and pulled it up to my opening. Pell didn't need a second invitation. He gripped my waist with one powerful hand, and slowly moved forward, pressing his swollen cock into me.

. . .

The initial pain was immense, and my vision flashed white as his thickness stretched me out. I thought I was going to go cross-eyed from how big he was. I grasped at the furs spread out on the floor, balling them up in my fists as I fought to keep it together.

"You okay?" Pell asked. "Should I stop?"

Reeling from the pain but wanting him to get all the way in, I grunted at him that if he stopped now, I'd straight up bite him on the dick.

He took his time with me, pushing his length in one inch at a time. The pain was mixing with pleasure now, as his cock pushed up against my inner spot. Tears came to my eyes, and I couldn't hold back a strained cry from escaping between gritted teeth.

Then he was all the way in, the aching fullness of his cock taking up every bit of me. It was the most incredible thing I'd ever felt—until he started to move his hips. I cried out as he rocked in and out of me, his cock slamming deep inside. Pell gripped me tight, his lips pulled back in a grimace of pleasure. His muscles bulged and tightened. Veins lined his arms, and I could almost see the vision of his hulking bear form shadowed behind him. He was so big and so powerful, and I fucking loved it. The pain had completely dissipated now, replaced only by rolling waves of pleasure. I was completely losing control of myself. I moaned loudly, a line of drool dripping down my chin as my eyes rolled back.

"I'm going to come," Pell growled, just as I felt myself reaching the edge. He fucked me even harder now, his cock reaching new depths. Climax hit me, sending stars shooting across my vision. I lost control, and convulsions of pleasure rocked through my entire body. I slumped onto the floor, unable to support myself. I felt Pell's cock swell up inside me as he thrust in one last time, bellowing out a loud roar that shook the walls of the cabin.

* * *

The cabin was empty when I slipped out from under my furs the next morning. A note sat on the table that said "Hunting." I wrapping myself up in the jacket I'd used the previous day, I opened the front door and was greeted by a gust of snowy wind. I quickly shut the door and got a fire going in the fireplace.

An hour later, Pell came back with two dead pheasants in his hands. "This was all I could get," he said. "Nearly impossible to see out there right now. It's like walking through fog." He set the pheasants down on the table next to his computer. "I thought the weather would be clearing up by now."

"Need help?" I asked.

"Sure. Do you know to pluck a bird?"

. . .

"Not yet," I said.

Things felt almost normal, and if it weren't for the new soreness that I had, I would've believed that what'd happened the night before had just been a dream. I wondered if Pell was going to bring it up, or if I should, and then realized that I was okay with leaving things alone. What had happened between us didn't mean anything, and I hadn't expected it to. After all, Pell was an attractive alpha, I was a good-looking omega, and we were stuck alone together in the middle of nowhere. I'd be lying if I said doing it hadn't always been in the back of my mind, especially after Pell's special bear treatment. It wouldn't be long until I'd be on my way, on to the next part of my journey.

What a way to start it, I thought, and smiled.

Pell eyed me. "What are you smiling about?"

"Nothing," I replied, and the smallest hint of a knowing smile flickered across his lips.

He showed me how to pluck the pheasants, and we stood at the kitchen counter silently working away. There were a few times when Pell interrupted me, placing his hands on mine to correct my technique. I again wondered how he felt about what we'd done, and if he'd say anything about it, but he didn't. I also wondered if Pell would want to do it again, but I was too nervous to make any kind of move. Yeah, I'd be leaving as soon as the weather let up, but it didn't mean we couldn't continue to enjoy each other's company now that the wolf was out of the den.

The phone hanging on the wall below a pair of deer antlers started to ring. Pell cursed, quickly washed his hands, and went to pick it up.

"Hello, this is Doctor Pell Darkclaw speaking." Pell's expression quickly became serious. He turned away to face the wall. "When did this happen?" He listened, nodding. "What have you tried? I understand. Yeah." He walked to the window and looked outside. "I'll be there as soon as I can."

After slamming the phone back into its cradle, Pell hurried over to the closet and pulled out a set of clothes and a backpack. I stared after him, a fist full of feathers in one hand and a half-plucked pheasant in the other.

"There's an emergency at the clinic I work at in Houndsville," he said. "They need my help."

"What happened?"

"A young boy fell into a frozen pond. He was pulled out in time, but he's still unconscious. He's just barely hanging on.

They think that one of my bear healing techniques might be able to save him."

"The weather?" It was still snowing furiously.

Pell gritted his teeth and started to strip out of his clothes, down to his skintight shifter wear. "If I wait around for it to become safe, it'll be too late. He needs me." He draped the backpack around his neck. "In my bear form, I'll be okay."

"I'll come with you."

He frowned. "No, you'll stay here. If something happens to you, I won't be able to carry you the whole way like last time."

"Nothing will happen to me. Last time I got spooked, and it won't happen again... Besides, this way I can get back into town."

"It's not a good idea. There's a boy's life on the line."

"I understand that. I won't slow you down. You saw me running the trials. You know I can take care of myself."

. . .

He stared at me, his crimson eyes searching mine. Then he nodded. "Hurry."

I quickly undressed, and Pell tossed me an extra pack. I stuffed my clothes and a winter jacket into the bag while Pell put the pheasants into the freezer.

"Prepare yourself," he said. "The way back is long, and it's going to be very cold."

I nodded. "Don't worry."

We burst out of the cabin, our bodies transforming the moment we hit the snow. Delicate feet shifted into toughened paws, cold sensitive skin erupted with shaggy winter fur, and senses heightened to find our way. Snow immediately began to collect in Pell's chestnut fur, making it look like he'd been speckled with white paint.

"Stay close," he said, his breath turning to thick vapor.

I was eager to show him that he had nothing to worry about. The only reason why he'd had to rescue me before was because I'd allowed myself to get frightened and lose my wits. That was not going to happen again—ever. I was Vander Luna, son of the Crescent Moon Pack. I wasn't weak.

. . .

Pell took off into a shambling run, kicking up huge plumes of snow with his gigantic paws as he went. I bounded after him, easily matching his speed. I was much lighter and much more agile than he was, and I ran elegantly on top of the snow.

The air was frigid cold, and it completely numbed my sense of smell. The wind was thick with snow, making it difficult to see where we were going, and the snow-covered trees made our surroundings look endlessly the same. It wasn't long before Pell's coat looked nearly as white as my own.

We kept at a steady run for as long as our stamina could hold out, which was a lot shorter due to the deep snow. The wind was howling through the trees, and it bit through my winter coat. I could see why Pell hadn't wanted us to go out in this weather. I pushed on at a brisk trot, determined not to let my growing concern show. I had no idea where we were. I couldn't catch a single scent, or hear anything except the sound of the wind. My energy was draining fast, and I could tell that Pell's was too. I stayed right at his side, worried that if I moved too slowly he'd disappear from my sight.

This is insane, I thought. I was about to ask Pell if we were okay, but the look I saw burning in his eyes shut me up. I could see he had no fear at all. Nothing was going to stop him from reaching town to help that little boy.

The deep snow became more and more difficult to walk through, even for me. Pell struggled, his massive weight forcing him to power through like a snowplow. He lost his balance and tumbled over, and I shouldered him back to his feet. I pushed myself up against his body to knock as much heavy snow as I could from his fur, and we soldiered on. I stayed by his side, doing my best to keep him supported. Neither of us spoke a word until Pell said, "We're nearly there."

Sure enough, I could see the break in the trees ahead, and beyond that, the twinkling of lights from the trailer park. I couldn't hold back an excited howl. We'd made it. I was back in civilization. One step closer to getting back on the road.

One step closer to parting ways with my rescuer.

* * *

We trudged through the snow, the top of the stone wall bordering the edge of Houndsville and forest just barely peeking up through the white. We climbed over it, and ran through the snow-covered town towards the clinic. We were greeted in the lobby by an older woman wearing a white doctor's coat.

Pell and I shifted back, and as our fur became skin again, clumps of snow slipped down our bodies and dropped into wet piles on the tile floor. We were both shivering.

"I'll get you towels," the woman said.

. . .

"How is he?" Pell asked, following her. I hurried along behind them.

"He's hanging in there, barely. I've done everything I can to stabilize him, but he's slipping. He was in the water for a long time." She lowered her voice. "I wanted to exhaust every option we have, but I'm losing confidence. Tell me there's something from your training that can help him."

She handed towels to Pell and I, and we quickly dried off before changing into our clothes.

"I'll give it everything I've got," Pell said, lips drawn into a thin line. "Vander, you should wait—"

"Let me watch," I said. "I won't get in the way."

Pell eyed me and then replied with the slightest nod. He turned and started to the examination room.

"Vander, this is Dr. Helena Elpaw, she owns the clinic."

She gave my hand a quick shake and turned to fall into step alongside Pell. I followed behind them. My heart pounded with nervous excitement, the same way it had before the start of the trials.

. . .

"Who is he?" I heard Dr. Elpaw ask Pell in a low voice.

"I'll explain later," Pell said. We hurried down the hall under sterile fluorescent lights.

The clinic's workers nodded to Pell as we passed by them. One said, "Thank you, Doctor Darkclaw." I could see just how respected he was by everyone here.

Dr. Elpaw stopped outside a closed door. "This one," she said, and Pell pushed it open.

Inside, a young boy, still in his wolf pup form, lay tucked under a blanket on an examination bed. His eyes were closed, and his breaths were so shallow it almost seemed like he wasn't breathing at all. A woman stood next to him, stroking his fur. The whole scene made my heart hurt.

Standing at the other side of the boy's bed was a short, thin man with dark hair and yellow eyes. From the scrubs he wore, I guessed he was a nurse. He turned, and when he saw Pell his eyes lit up.

"Thank you for coming, Dr. Darkclaw," he said, with clear relief in his voice.

. . .

Pell nodded at him. If he was worried, it didn't show in his face at all. Actually, it was the opposite. Pell was exuding a whole new level of strength and confidence I hadn't seen back at the cabin. He looked like he was capable of doing anything.

"Doctor Darkclaw," the woman said, her eyes red with tears. "Please help him. Please tell me there's something you can do."

"I'm going to do everything I can," Pell said.

She hugged him. "He's my only son," she said, her voice trembling.

"I know, and I'm not going to give up on Rian, okay? Now, if you could go with Michael out to the waiting room."

She nodded. "Please take care of him." Then she followed the nurse out of the room.

"This is going to be difficult," Pell said to me. "I can have someone set you up in the motel…"

"I won't get in your way," I repeated. "Please."

. . .

I wanted to see him working. I wanted to see his passion, his skills. But most of all, I wanted to see him save that boy's life.

He turned to Dr. Elpaw. "Doctor," he said, and she nodded. They both started to shift, stopping in partial wolf and bear forms. Pell's face had morphed so it looked like a bear's head on a human's body, and Dr. Elpaw was the same.

Pell lowered his nose to the boy, sniffing carefully at his fur. He did this for about five minutes before going to the wall, where there was a set of cabinet-sized double doors. Tendrils of vapor curled out when he opened them, revealing rows of shelves stocked with a variety of living plants, jars of liquid of different colors, bottles of powder, boxes of pills, and even cages with what looked like insects. With a pair of small silver scissors, he selectively clipped some leaves from one of the plants. Then he chose a bottle of red powder, a bottle of white powder, and a box of small white crystals, and brought them all over to the counter.

Pell worked silently, combining portions of the ingredients as Dr. Elpaw stood by and watched him. Occasionally he would ask for something, and Dr. Elpaw would quickly go and retrieve it. He used a mortar and pestle to grind the mixture up, stopping every ten seconds or so to bring it to his nose.

"How's Rian doing?" Pell asked, and Dr. Elpaw went over to the boy and sniffed his ear, nose and neck.

. . .

"Not looking good," she said. "Pell, if you don't get this mixture right, I don't think you're going to get another shot. We've already used up so much time."

He nodded gravely. "I know."

Come on, Pell, I thought. *You can do this. You can save him.* The pressure he felt must've been immense, but he worked with calm focus and precision. I was watching a master at work, fighting a battle of life and death, and it was awe-inspiring to see.

It was at that moment that I had a sudden realization, and I truly understood what my brother-in-law had told me the night of the FAS trials. *This is true strength.*

Then I realized something else, something even more startling—I realized how I felt about Pell.

PELL

It was Rian, Cherry Windheart's little boy. He'd gone out with some friends to the frozen pond on the west side of town, and fallen through thin ice. Despite my warnings, he'd been in his wolf form, and his leg had still not fully healed. He hadn't been able to swim with his injury.

I wasn't going to let him die.

On the journey into town, I'd wracked my brain trying to figure out what mixture of components would be the right one to bring the boy back to us. There were thousands of possible combinations and ratios, and I knew it would be vital that I got it right on the first try. There wasn't time for mistakes.

I found my mind going back to my early training with my dad, when he'd brought me out into the winter forest and showed me the various natural growing herbs and roots that made up the medicines commonly used during the winter.

"The patient's stature, vitality and animal energy all come into play when concocting a medicine," he'd told me. "You need to be keen to all of them, and a bear's senses are the most capable of performing that task."

I was certain that I'd gotten the mixture right. I couldn't afford to doubt myself.

I took the pulverized powder and scraped it into the mixer, which would infuse it into a serum that could be injected into Rian's bloodstream. The machine hummed to life, and a pink liquid began to drip into an IV bag. I stepped over to Rian's side and placed my nose against his neck, checking his vitals. His body temperature was still dropping, and his pulse was down to a crawl. Helena and I exchanged a glance.

The machine buzzed. Helena was waiting, and she retrieved the bag and connected it up to a line, and then handed the IV to me. I hung the bag on the pole next to the bed, and then quickly pushed the needle into Rian's arm where the fur had already been shaved away. I let out a long sigh.

"The effects should come fairly quickly, whether they're good or bad," I said. "We just have to wait."

. . .

DOCTOR TO THE OMEGA

Helena brought Mrs. Windheart back into the room, and we all stood by the bed, waiting for any changes. *I did it perfectly,* I told myself. *He's going to be fine. He's going to recover.*

I looked over at Vander. He seemed to be lost in thought.

Even though he'd volunteered to follow me back to town, I'd been reluctant to let him come. Yeah, I knew he was capable and stronger than most, but I'd been afraid. I wanted to keep him safe. And more than that… I didn't want him to leave.

That was something I didn't think I'd be able to admit to him, even after what we'd done together. Even after letting my desire for him overpower all reason. Regardless of how I felt, I knew that him leaving was the best thing he could do. He was only starting on his journey. There was nothing for him here.

I knew without a doubt it would hurt when he left. Vander had ignited something in me I'd never felt for anyone before, and it'd come from out of nowhere. I could deal with it, though. I was dedicated to my work, and I'd gone this long being by myself. Bears were solitary by nature. Given time, I'd move on from this.

After ten minutes, I pressed my nose to Rian's neck again. *No changes. No difference.* I reminded myself that no change was better than a negative one.

. . .

Ten minutes after that, I checked him again. Helena and I exchanged another private glance, not wanting to let our worry show be detected by Mrs. Windheart. I hadn't expected a reaction to the medicine to take this long.

I did everything perfectly, I reminded myself. *Questioning it will not help the situation.*

Helena left to go attend to other patients. Later, Michael brought us dinner. Vander was doing his best not to doze off. Cherry stayed attentive by Rian's side.

Then, nearly five hours after administering the medicine, Rian woke up.

"Doctor," Cherry said, her voice raising with surprise. "Doctor!"

I was standing at the counter, re-evaluating my choices for the medication for probably the hundredth time. I turned around and saw Rian stirring on the bed. His ears twitched, and his eyes had opened into tight slits. I hurried over. Vander stood up from his chair.

"I'll go get Dr. Elpaw," Michael said, and rushed out of the room.

. . .

Slowly, Rian's body shifted until he was finally back in his human form. His skin was clammy and pale, and his eyes were glassy and sluggishly gazed up at us. I pressed my nose to his neck. His pulse felt strong. I could smell the energy returning to him.

"Mrs. Windheart, I think Rian is going to be okay," I said.

Helena and Michael returned back to the room, and Helena gave me a look of relieved amazement. I was surprised to feel an affectionate touch on my arm. It was Vander. I looked at him, and he quickly pulled his hand away and stuffed it into his pocket.

"Doctor... Darkclaw?" Rian whispered in a tiny, barely-there voice. "Mom?"

Cherry kissed his hand, tears streaming down her cheeks. "I'm here, Rian. Mommy is here."

"How do you feel, Rian?" I asked, kneeling down beside him.

He gazed at me, blinking slowly. "You look funny," he said, and raised a hand up to touch my head, which I'd forgotten was shifted partially into my bear form. He squeezed my bear's ears, and smiled. Everyone laughed. "What happened?" he asked.

. . .

"You had an accident," I told him.

"Dr. Darkclaw saved you," Cherry said.

"And Dr. Elpaw, and Nurse Chestnut," I said. "Everyone was very worried about you, Rian."

"I'm sorry," he said.

"Don't worry about a thing. Just rest." I stood up. "Speaking of rest, I think that's what I need right now."

"I'll give The Dog's Bark a call," Michael said helpfully. "Two rooms?"

"Yes, thank you."

"I can take care of my own room, thanks," Vander said.

After Michael left, I asked Vander to go to the waiting room while I finished taking care of Rian. I got out a pad of paper and started to write down the formula I'd used to make the medication so that Helena or one of the nurses could make more of it to continue to give to the boy until he'd fully recovered.

. . .

"I knew I could count on you," Helena said, leaning against the counter. "So. Who is he?"

"A patient," I said.

She laughed. "Okay. And?"

"I found him lost and injured in the woods attempting to walk to Diamond Dust. I told him I'd help him find a ride there in town.

"So, you nursed him back to health and gave him a place to stay during the storm. How romantic."

"I don't know what you're talking about."

"Come on, Pell. You're not hiding anything. I've know you too well. I could tell there was something going on between the two of you the moment you stepped through the front door. And you should've seen the way he was looking at you while you were working." She huffed a chuckle. "So, spill the honey."

There was obviously no hiding anything from the old wolf. "Okay, okay," I said. "It's nothing serious. Like I said, I was going to help him get a ride to Diamond Dust from town. And we're here, so, that's it."

. . .

She gave me a look. "Pell, forgive me for being nosy, but never once in the time that I've known you have I ever seen you with someone. This is a first, this is big. Now, my intuition is telling me that there's a little more to this than just 'nothing serious.' I think having someone in your life would be good, don't you?"

"It's nothing serious," I said. "Besides, when would I have the time to dedicate to a relationship? I've got the three clinics and my job. No, there's too much that I need to do."

"You told me about how your parents feel about you working out here," Helena said. "Does that have anything to do with it? Because he's a wolf?"

"No," I said, a little more harshly than I'd intended. "It doesn't." I finished writing the last bit of the formula and tore off the paper. "Don't worry about me."

"Stay in town," she said. "I'll compensate your room and board. You're my best healer on staff, I want you around for the rest of this bad weather. Who knows what else might happen."

"Sure."

. . .

"Do me another favor?"

"What?"

"Don't send that omega away just yet."

"It's not up to me, Helena. He's on his own journey. Once a way to Diamond Dust comes through, he'll hit the road."

Helena crossed her arms over her chest. It looked like she had something more to say, but she kept it to herself. "Good work today," she said. "I'll take care of it from here. Get some rest. You were out in the cold for a long time. I don't want my best doctor getting sick."

I smiled and handed her the formula. "Goodnight."

Michael and Vander were waiting in the lobby. "Got it all sorted out for you, Dr. Darkclaw," Michael said. "They're waiting for you over at The Dog's Bark."

Vander and I pulled on our warm coats and left the clinic. It was dark out, and a cold wind kicked up whirls of snow that sparkled like fairy dust under the orange glow of flickering streetlights. I suddenly felt exhausted. The day was finally catching up with me.

. . .

Thankfully, The Dog's Bark was just a short walk down the street from the clinic. Vander walked along beside me, and I found myself wanting to move closer to him. I wanted to take his hand into mine, and feel the warmth of his skin. I'd been stubborn with Helena, but the truth still remained sharp in my mind—I didn't want him to leave. I was happy to stay in town where I could be with him for a little longer until he was gone. And how long until that would happen? A day? Two days? With the fresh snow, there would be plenty of people passing through Houndsville to get up to Diamond Dust to do some skiing. It wouldn't be long before Vander left with one of them.

Then I could move on with my life.

I felt a twinge of sadness grip my heart at the thought. *Move on*. It was nothing serious, so why did I feel so hurt about it? All we did was indulge in our urges. Any man and any alpha would have. It didn't mean anything more than that.

Right?

Vander and I had rooms next to each other, and we said goodnight and separated. I flipped on the heater and immediately stripped off my clothes to go jump into the shower. I made the water as hot as I could bear, and the bathroom filled with steam. The water felt amazing, just what I needed to cut through the chill and soothe my muscles, which were sore from the journey into town.

. . .

Afterwards, I wrapped myself up in a towel and lay down on the bed. Typically, after a difficult procedure I would go over everything in my mind to try and see what I could improve on, but right now, the first thing that came to my head was Vander.

Letting him go wouldn't be a problem, I decided. There was no reason it should be. We'd fucked once. That was it. I'd had hookups before, and there was no reason this one should be anything different. And yet, it was different. I was drawn to him in a way I'd never been with anyone else.

A knock on the door dividing our rooms bolted me upright. I opened it.

"I didn't wake you up, did I?" Vander asked.

I told him he hadn't, and invited him into my room.

"What you did today was amazing," he said, sitting on the edge of my bed. He wore one of the motel's bathrobes, and his hair was damp from a shower. "It really opened my eyes to what you do."

"We were lucky today," I said. "I was able to save the boy's life. It's not always like that, no matter how good you are or how much you know."

. . .

Vander nodded. "You seemed perfectly in control, though. I could see how confident everyone became when you arrived."

I smiled. "I've had just as much practice hiding my fears as I have treating people."

"I'm glad that I was there. Thank you for letting me stay to watch."

"Sure," I said.

An awkward silence passed between us.

"I was wondering," Vander said, looking adorably sheepish, "if you need to examine me."

I blinked. The truth was that Vander's injuries were past the point of needing to be examined—they were healing up nicely, and barring him doing anything extreme to reinjure himself, they would be fine.

"Yeah," I said. "I can do that for you."

Almost eagerly, Vander stood up, faced his back to me and pulled off his robe. He was naked underneath, and I felt my cock pulse to life. His casual willingness to be naked around me turned me on. I sat on the edge of the bed behind him and began the examination.

I ran my finger up along his leg, tracing the now scabbed over wound, and reached his gorgeous ass. As memories of the night before ran through my mind, my ability to suppress my growing erection slipped away. I wanted to touch him like I had and continue whatever this silent, secret thing we had between us was.

I was able to keep myself in check. I reached the end of the wound, and told him that everything looked good. He stood there silently, unmoving for a moment. Then he turned around.

Vander looked down at me with his ice-blue eyes, his cock fully erect and standing tall right in front of my face. His gaze begged me to take him, and all my defenses immediately crumbled into dust.

I raked my fingers down his front, rising and falling over his muscles like a roller coaster. When they reached the bottom of his abs, I reached around and grabbed hold of his ass, pulling him in closer. I pressed my lips up to the head of his cock and kissed it, lapping up the bead of honey that dripped from the tip. Vander shivered and grabbed my wrists to stabilize himself as I pulled him into my mouth, gulping every inch of him down my throat.

. . .

I repeatedly teased him by bringing him close to the edge with my tongue and my lips, backing off at the last moment. Then I stood up and dropped my towel to the floor. I pulled him into a deep kiss, our cocks rubbing stiffly against one another. Vander wrapped his hands around both of them, squeezing them together and stroking them as our tongues probed into each other's mouths. I couldn't get enough of his lips.

Then, I had him on the bed, his legs pushed back so his knees touched his shoulders. I took my middle and ring fingers and swirled them around his opening, which had grown wet with excitement. Vander's cock twitched in reaction.

"Oh, fuck," he sighed as I pushed my fingers all the way inside of him.

I massaged and stretched him out as I rubbed his cock with my free hand until he was begging me to give him the real thing, and I was more than willing to comply. I quickly slipped on a condom.

My cock pressed up against his opening, and when I pushed forward I nearly came right then and there from how incredibly tight he was. I took it slow at first, but Vander was eager and pushed me to fuck him harder and faster.

Soon I was slamming into him, and the bed creaked and pounded loudly against the wall. I had to do everything in my power not to come. Vander reached down and started to stroke himself, begging me not to stop.

"I can't hold on," I grunted. "Oh, *shit*, it feels so good."

I was fucking him so hard, I thought the bed might smash right through the damn wall.

Vander's eyes widened and his mouth dropped open into a silent moan. He gripped the blankets with one hand and kept cranking away at his cock with the other. I felt him tighten around me.

"I'm… gonna come!" he grunted.

I let myself go, pushing in all the way just as Vander's cock released, spurting up all over his chest. The orgasm struck me like a freight train, and I couldn't hold back a roar as my seed filled up the condom. Stars danced around my head. I slowly withdrew from him, and then collapsed onto the bed next to him.

Vander lay there, his legs slowly lowering down to the bed with the occasional twitch. "*Fuck*," he sighed.

"Let me clean you up," I said through heavy breaths, and licked his load off of his chest. It was as delicious as honey.

Then he kissed me, licking what remained from my lips. A shiver ran through my body as I wrapped my arms around him and pulled him close. I couldn't believe how good being with him felt.

How could I tell him I didn't want him to go?

It turned out, I wouldn't have to.

Vander traced his finger along the ridge of my pec and circled it around my nipple. "We should talk about this thing we have going on," he said.

"Whatever it is that we have will be gone once you leave," I said. "So, it's probably best we don't."

He looked at me. "That's part of what I want to talk to you about, Pell," he said. "I… I'm not leaving."

"What?"

"I'm going to stay. With you, if you're willing. In town, if you're not. Either way, I want to stay here and watch you work, and maybe even learn how to become a healer."

"You're joking," I said.

. . .

"No. Seeing you save that boy's life today woke something in me. It made me realize what I want to fight for. I want the strength that you have. To strength to try and help people, even if you might fail."

"You want to stay here with me?" I asked, completely stunned.

"Yes," he said. "And... I want to continue with this thing we have."

"So," I said, cracking just the slightest smile. "Just what is this thing that we have?"

"I don't know," he replied. "You were the one who started it. Why don't you tell me what it is?"

"Well," I said. "Honestly, it took me by surprise. It just kind of happened, but I'd be lying if I said it hasn't grabbed hold of me. I'm just kind of going for the ride right now. What do you think?"

"That basically described the entire week for me," Vander said, grinning. "One crazy ride."

. . .

"An adventure," I suggested. "Just what you wanted."

"Yeah. And I'm on board to see where this ride takes us."

* * *

Helena grinned up at me from behind her desk. "You want my permission for Vander to shadow you at the clinic," she repeated. "Fine. You don't need to ask me about something like that."

"Thanks," I said.

"So. Nothing serious, huh? I guess a lot can change over the span of twelve hours."

"Okay, okay. So, there's something. But I'm not going to say it's serious. It's just something."

"The fact that you're seeing someone is serious enough to me," she said, the grin still stuck on her face. "I promise I won't pry about it—much. But I'm happy for you."

Vander was waiting for me outside in the lobby, sitting amongst the people waiting for their turn to be seen. He looked at me hopefully.

. . .

"You're good to go," I said. "You're sure you want to do this?"

"Positive," he said, getting up to follow me into the back. "In fact, it's pretty incredible. I don't think I've felt this strong about something since I first decided I wanted to study at the FAS."

"You can't become a real healer just by watching me work for a little while. It'll take years of dedicated study at a proper school, or under a master. But I can expose you to this life and to the demands it'll place on you, and we can find out if you're up to the challenge. That's what I can offer you."

"Okay, I understand."

We stopped outside of Rian's examination room, where we'd had him stay for the night, recovering. A nurse passed by and nodded a greeting to me. I waited until she was around the corner and out of sight before taking Vander into my arms. He seemed surprised at first, and then relaxed into my embrace.

"When I first met you, I was impressed by how you put yourself on the line to save another person's life. I gave you my card hoping that maybe you'd change your mind about being a fighter, but honestly, I never really believed that our paths would cross again after that day. It's hard for me to express my feelings. I just want you to know how happy I am that you're here. I'm not the type who readily believes in things like destiny, but... um..." I couldn't find the words to finish. Everything I wanted to say sounded so silly when I tried it out in my head.

Maybe we were fated to meet? Maybe we were meant to be together? Maybe I was falling hard for someone for the first time in my life and I didn't know how to deal with it?

"I understand," Vander said. "I think I was meant to be come here, and to meet you again."

Footsteps sounded from around the corner, and the two of us stepped away from each other, breaking our hug. Meant to be together, but not ready for the world to know—at least I wasn't.

Rian was awake and being visited by the group of friends who'd been out with him when he'd fallen through the ice. He was making a speedy recovery, and I told his mother that he could leave the clinic that day.

"About payment..." she said nervously.

"Dr. Elpaw knows and understands your situation," I said softly. "Don't worry. Speak to her, and she'll take care of you."

. . .

"Thank you, Doctor," she said.

"Mrs. Windheart can barely afford to feed and clothe her boy," I explained to Vander, later. "It's the same with many of the people who live in the small towns outside of the city. It's not a situation many folks from the big city clans see on a daily basis, but it's real."

"And you guys do your work for free?" Vander asked.

"We are all volunteers," I said. "We donate our time. Dr. Elpaw's clinics operate mostly on donations. She's well connected back in Wolfheart, and gets donations from some very wealthy people. It's how we stay in operation."

"How many clinics are there?"

"Three. Houndsville, Pinetown and Forest Ridge."

"You go between all three?" he asked, looking shocked. "And you work for HeliHound? How do you do it?"

"My work with HeliHound is by contract," I said. "I'll have weeks away from the job, sometimes. Mostly, I spend my time between the clinics."

. . .

Vander nodded. "You're amazing, Pell. Your dedication is so inspiring. Now I finally understand why you haven't been able to go back home for the Food Gathering in so long. To be honest, I was beginning to wonder if you've been avoiding Ursidcomb."

"No," I said quickly. "Winter is the busiest time of the year, and now you've seen first-hand why that is."

"Your parents must be proud of you for what you do here. For bringing your skills to so many people who really need it."

"I don't know if 'proud' is the exactly the word I'd use," I said. "They don't exactly get it. Like I told you, my family has run a clinic in Ursidcomb for generations. I'm the first to have dropped the mantle of taking over the place. They'd much rather have me back there than out here."

"Maybe if they saw the work you were doing, they'd understand."

"No," I said, "I don't think so. My parents... we don't see eye to eye on much at all, really. I gave up trying to win them over a long time ago. Now it's just better if I avoid them altogether. It saves us all a lot of hard feelings."

. . .

"But you must miss them, at least a little. I couldn't imagine being completely separated from my family."

"Well, we're a bit different," I said. "They could care less about what I'm doing, if it doesn't involve coming back to Ursidcomb and being the son they want me to be."

"So… you are avoiding Ursidcomb?"

I sighed. "Why are we talking about this?"

Vander shrugged, and dropped the topic.

I immediately felt bad, both for snapping at him and because in all honesty, yes, I did miss my home and my family.

It would mean the world to me if they could finally see why I'd left, and acknowledge that all of my hard work was honoring our family traditions and not shunning them. I wished they could be more open minded. But the ties had been cut. I already knew that if I went back now, after what had happened between my father and I, all I'd receive would be disappointment, and I couldn't deal with that.

Pride was a terrible thing.

VANDER

I worked alongside Pell, absorbing everything I could. After just four days, it'd come to the point where I could do a basic check-up on a patient and diagnose some of the typical winter illnesses. I'd never been taught to use my wolf nose in that way before, pressing it up to the patient's neck or ears to sniff out their vitals. At first, my senses were weak and couldn't detect anything at all, whereas Pell seemed to be able to tell everything about the patient with a single whiff. It was an amazing feeling when I finally was able to get the faintest scent of blood pumping through veins.

"Eventually, you'll be able to tell how fast their heart is beating. You'll be able to smell viruses and disease in the bloodstream. The best healers are those with the most sensitive noses. It's a big part of the reason why bears are such good healers. My father can pinpoint cancer in a patient just by standing at their bedside. He even can tell what medications were given to someone. I'm good, but I'm still a long way away from that."

I could hear the admiration Pell had for his father in the way he spoke about him. I remembered the book I'd found on his shelf, and the photograph inside of it. Pell had been going back home for the Food Gathering festival until two years ago, when something big had happened that'd made him decide not to return home again. He wanted me to believe that he didn't want to see his parents again, that he hated them. I wasn't convinced that was true.

I could've dropped it, but I was curious. More than that, I sensed that Pell did want to go home. He did want to see his parents again, and celebrate the Food Gathering festival with them. Thinking about never seeing my family again made me sad. Sure, Mom was single-minded, prissy and sometimes could care more about family status than anything else. Dad was cold and could treat my favorite brother like shit. And my brothers all had their annoying quirks, even Loch. But they were my family, and I loved them. I couldn't imagine cutting them out from my life, no matter what happened.

And Pell loved his family. I'd heard it in his voice when he talked about the Gathering, and when he spoke about his mom's cooking. I heard it when he talked about his dad.

Now that I'd decided to stay on with Pell for the remainder of my trip, my feelings for him had started to grow in a way I hadn't expected. I admired him and was completely in awe of his strength and dedication and generosity. I was falling hard for him. How could I not want to do something, knowing that he was hurting inside? He'd done so much for me in the short time we'd known each other—he'd saved my life twice, and he'd shown me a new path in life I would never have decided to walk down before. I wanted to help him, to repay him in some small way.

I knew that the Food Gathering Festival was coming up at the end of the month. I realized that I needed to find a way to convince Pell to go back home and see his family again. I wanted to bring him that closure.

* * *

I raised the beaker of crushed green powder up to my nose, which I'd shifted into its wolf form, and took a deep inhale of it.

"I'd say… about half a gram of silwart, mixed with three-eighths of a gram of silver dust, and less than one-twelfth a gram of dark tricopal."

Pell nodded, and smiled. "Color me impressed, Vander. It was livstone, and not dark tricopal, but you got the measurements just about spot on. You're picking this up fast, especially for a wolf."

"I always get those two mixed up," I said.

"For a week of study, it's amazing."

"How long did it take you to be able to measure medicine?"

"A day for the basics. Three to really get a hang of it. But bears have a natural advantage, so it's pointless to compare." He wrapped his arm around me and kissed me on the forehead. "I'm really proud of you. If you apply yourself like this with real, dedicated instruction… I'm sure you'll go far."

There was a knock on the door of the examination room. Pell dropped his hand to his side as Michael peeked his head inside.

"Dr. Darkclaw, Mr. Grezl is here for his appointment. Room five."

"Thank you, Michael. Let him know I'll be there in a moment."

Despite our growing relationship, Pell and I still were not public about it. I was sure that people around the clinic aside from Dr. Elpaw knew Pell and I were involved—there had been a few not-so-discreet slipups—but Pell seemed to want to keep things on the down low. Keeping things professional in the clinic was perfectly understandable, but even when we walked to and from The Dog's Bark, or went for food in town, Pell kept the public displays of affection to a minimum.

I quickly learned that Pell wasn't the kind of person who vocalized his feelings about things like this easily. He didn't make any kind of specific request to keep things on the down-low, it just was that way. And it wasn't that he was shy. I just got the sense that he wasn't used to having romantic feelings for someone. Given what a workaholic he was, it wasn't too much of a surprise. It was kind of cute at first, but I'd started to wonder if our "thing" would ever become serious enough to stop being hidden.

Or was this as far as our ride would go?

"Mr. Grezl has been my patient since I first started here," Pell told me.

He pushed open the door to examination room five, and when I saw the man who was sitting on the bed, I froze. An icy chill went through my body as his red eyes met mine.

It was the grizzled wolf who'd watched me in the trailer park that first day in Houndsville. The one I was certain had stalked me in the woods.

"'Afternoon, Mr. Grezl," said Pell. "This is my assistant, Vander Luna. He'll be helping with your examination today. So, what's going on?"

I cautiously went into the room and pressed my back against the door, my defenses raised.

"Just the usual," he said, his voice rough and gravelly. He touched his throat. "Nasty cough that I can't rid of. And the cold is making my condition worse. Aggravating every damn thing."

"Are you still puffing on those cigarettes?" Pell asked.

"Yeah."

"Well, that'd explain the cough."

"I know, Doctor, I've tried to give them up. On the plus side, I only smoke outside now, like you instructed." He eyed me. "I'm sorry. Have I met you before?" He broke out in a fit of wheezy coughs. "One of my son's friends, maybe?"

"No," I said tensely. Pell looked at me inquisitively.

He clapped his hands together. "Oh shit. I remember! You were wandering around the neighborhood about a week past. Hounds of Hell, I can't believe I remembered that. Are you new to the neighborhood? Are we neighbors?"

. . .

"And you followed me into the woods," I said flatly.

Mr. Grezl looked surprised. "Followed you? I don't think so."

"You chased after me."

Pell looked back and forth between the two of us, and then started to laugh. "Hold on a second. Vander, you think Mr. Grezl was the one who chased you through the woods?"

"No, I don't think that was me."

"Like I told you," said Pell. "It was probably a wild boar."

"Oh, territorial buggers, those are," Mr. Grezl agreed.

"There's a simple explanation for why it couldn't have been him," Pell went on.

Mr. Grezl slipped down from the examination bed, immediately sinking into a heavy limp. He shuffled slowly back and forth, holding his leg. "No chasing anyone for me. Not now or ever."

. . .

"Mr. Grezl was born with deformities in his bones which handicap his mobility," said Pell, matter-of-factly. "Even the medication I give to him only helps him move around the house."

I was starting to feel defensive. "You shifted into your wolf form when you saw me. Like you were going to come after me."

He nodded. "Yeah. I'm sorry it came off that way."

"Mr. Grezl also has a condition called involuntary shift syndrome," Pell said. "It causes him to randomly shift without control over when it occurs."

"I'm just a broken old wolf," Mr. Grezl said with a rough laugh that revealed a mouth full of crooked, yellow teeth. Then, suddenly, he shifted into his wolf form. "See?"

After I apologized a thousand times to Mr. Grezl, Pell showed me how to mix up some medicine that would help him control his shifting, and for his legs. Mr. Grezl was incredibly understanding and wasn't even upset that I'd accused him of stalking me. It was probably not the sort of thing someone would want to have happen during a visit to the healing clinic.

. . .

"I'm so sorry," I told Pell after Mr. Grezl had left. "What I did was very unprofessional…"

"Don't worry about it."

"You and the clinic have a reputation, and I don't want to screw that up. I feel so embarrassed."

"You shouldn't," he said. He took my hand in his, and butterflies fluttered around my stomach. "Look, I'm glad we were able to get that cleared up for you. I'm glad that you said something. If someone hurt you, even if they were one of my patients, I'd want to know. I could care less about my reputation. You're more important than that."

Pell turned away to his paperwork, leaving me standing there with a stupid grin on my face, the butterflies now doing all sorts of crazy moves. *I'm important to him,* I thought. It was amazing how something so small could mean so much to me.

Every moment I spent with him, watching him work, seeing how amazing he was, I only fell harder for him. Every compliment he gave me, every secret touch while we were working, every one of those moments made my heart go wild for him. I tried to convince myself that I was okay with our undefined relationship, but it quickly began to eat at me. I wanted to know if Pell felt the same way about me as I did about him.

. . .

I wanted us to be more.

* * *

After spending nine days in Houndsville, the weather finally calmed down. The sky cleared, the sun came out, and the day was warm enough for most of the town to come out and actually enjoy the fresh snowfall. The hills by the Northern Forest border were taken over by the town children, sliding down on their bellies in their wolf forms. The main street bustled with cars as people from Wolfheart passed through town on their way up to Diamond Dust and the freshly powdered mountains.

Sitting on the bed in his motel room, I slid my hands around Pell's naked waist, enjoying the feeling of his rippling abs beneath my fingertips. I kissed his back just below his shoulder blade, and then pressed my cheek against him.

"Pell?" I asked.

"Hm?"

"What happens now that the weather has cleared?"

He stood up, sliding out of my grasp, and started to get dressed to go to the clinic. "Well, I'll be able to pick up my rounds again. I'll need to go to the other clinics and take care of my patients there. I'll let Helena know that I'll no longer need the hotel room, now that the way back to the cabin is open."

"I see," I said. "What about us?"

"Us? Well, you'll come back to the cabin too, and you can continue to come with me."

"Okay, but... Pell, what are we?"

"How do you mean?"

"I mean, why do we pretend like we're not together when we're out in public? Why don't we decide what we mean to each other?"

"I thought we agreed that we were going along for the ride."

I frowned. "I am. But I'm starting to wonder where this ride is going and if you're even on the same ride that I'm on. I... really care about you, Pell." I wasn't able to use the word I really wanted to—I was too afraid. "I just want to know how you feel about me."

"I thought how I feel about you is obvious," he said. "I care about you."

. . .

"But not enough to be seen together in public."

"Why does that matter? We're together when we're alone, isn't that enough?"

"Because it feels like you're ashamed of being with me," I said. "Like you're hiding a casual relationship. Fuck, Pell. I just need to know if that's what this is. Because I'm falling way too hard for you, too quickly, for this to just be casual."

"Vander, I..." It looked like he was trying to find the right words to say but couldn't find them. "I don't know what to tell you."

"Pell, please," I begged him.

"I care about you," he said. "I really do. It's just... I don't... I don't know."

If he really cared about me, why couldn't he just tell me he wanted to be with me? That he wanted this to be a real relationship, one where we didn't have to hide things?

It was my own fault, for letting my feelings for him get out of hand. I should've known that he wouldn't want anything serious. Pell was dedicated to his work. It was obvious from the very start what his expectations for this relationship was. Begun in silence. Carried out in silence.

I nodded. "Okay," I said flatly. "I get it." Pell reached for my hand, and I moved it away.

"Vander?"

"I can't let this go any further," I said. "I've already let it go too far."

"Wait, Vander…" Pell grabbed me by the wrist, and I yanked my hand free.

"No, Pell," I said, fighting back tears. "I've fallen in love and been jerked around by alphas too many times in the past. I should've learned my lesson by now. I shouldn't have let you in so far."

I moved for the door. I needed to get out of here, to just forget about him and everything I felt for him. I was an idiot, a naïve idiot who always let himself get taken advantage of.

You knew how he felt about this and what this was, and you still let yourself get sucked in.

. . .

"Vander," Pell said, his voice raising. "Stop. Please, just wait." He grabbed my shoulder and, I knocked his arm away.

"Don't touch me," I growled. I couldn't stop the tears from streaming down my cheeks.

Pell stepped in front of the door, his huge body blocking it.

"Get out of my way," I said. "I'm leaving. I'm going home. Just get out of my way, Pell. Don't make me force you out of the way."

He shook his head. "Vander, listen to me…"

I'd had enough. I shifted, transforming into my half-wolf form, and barreled towards the door. I didn't care. I'd smash him through the damn thing if I had to. I just needed to get out of there, to get away before my heart completely shattered, because I'd somehow managed to fall head over paws in love with him.

"Vander!" Pell shouted. His clothes ripped to shreds as his body burst out in an explosion of muscle and fur. He spread his gigantic bear arms just as I slammed shoulder-first into him. But instead of smashing him through the door, I found myself flying backwards, wrapped up in a tight bear-hug. Pell and I crashed into the bed, completely pulverizing the frame.

. . .

I struggled against him, the tears still running down my fur covered face. "Let me go," I cried. "Just let me go."

"I'm not going to let you go," Pell said. "Because I love you. *I love you, Vander.*"

I froze.

"I love you," he repeated, like he was amazed to hear the words come out of his mouth. "I'm in love with you. I'm sorry. I'm sorry I couldn't say it before. I'm sorry I was so afraid. I've never felt this way about anyone before, and I didn't know how to deal with it. I was afraid to commit to you. But I need you, Vander. I want you to be with me. I never want this ride to end."

"Dammit, Pell," I sobbed. Slowly, I shifted back to my human form.

"I'm sorry," he said. He shifted back too, his naked body embracing mine. "I'm so sorry."

I lay there in his arms, the tears flowing from the overwhelming emotion I felt—the relief, sadness, the anger, and the love for him. He stroked my hair and kept me wrapped tightly in his strong arms.

PELL

I hadn't realized how much I loved him until the moment he was about to walk out the door and leave. Talk about a wake-up call. It was strange, like a part of my heart and my mind had been locked shut, and Vander had forced it open. Everything felt different.

Why had admitting that I loved him been so damn hard?

We made the walk back to the cabin in our wolf and bear forms, padding through powder snow gleaming like freshly polished diamonds. It was a completely different scene from when we'd come into town—birds flitted from branch to branch, rabbits dashed across the snow into their burrows, and clean sunlight glinted down through the trees.

. . .

"It's like an entirely different place," Vander said. "It's kind of amazing how something can be so hostile one day, and become so beautiful on another."

Vander and I worked together to dig out the front door of cabin, which had been piled with snow. Inside, we lit a fire and got the heater going to thaw out the cold that clung to every surface. Vander used my laptop to write a letter to his parents to update them on his situation.

"Did you tell them about us?" I asked.

"Of course," he said. "I'm looking forward to hearing my mom's reaction. She'd probably have a heart attack to know I'm with a bear."

"That's probably the last thing they'd expect to hear from you," I said, laughing.

"I don't know what they'll be more shocked about," he said. "That, or that I'm learning how to become a healer."

"Will they be angry?"

He shrugged. "I don't know. I love my parents, but I don't need their approval for everything I do. I've learned to care, but not care. If I hadn't, I'd probably have gone crazy a long time ago with all their expectations. In the end, they'll get over it."

I tried to imagine how my parents would react if I told them about Vander, and decided they'd probably be better off not knowing.

"I'm thinking of renting a place in town," Vander said. "I spoke with Dr. Elpaw, and she said she knew of a couple of places that were available in Houndsville."

"Why rent a place?" I asked. "You have a place to stay."

"I'm already asking a lot of you as it is," he said. "I don't want to burden you."

"Not at all, Vander," I said, squeezing his hand. "You're not at all a burden. You have no idea how happy it makes me to know that you want to learn how to be a healer—and that you're my man. I'd do anything to make you happy."

My heart fluttered. It felt amazing to be able to admit that to him. I wanted to share the entire world with him, and for the first time in my life I saw something other than my profession. It was something I'd never experienced before, and it felt freeing and incredibly wonderful. How could one man change me so much and so quickly? It didn't seem possible to feel this happy. It was like a cure to a sickness I hadn't even known I'd had.

He smiled and pressed his lips to mine. His kiss was like honey, delicious and irresistible, and I wanted more and more.

Vander decided he would continue to stay with me until after the Food Gathering festival at the end of the month, after which he'd make the decision about whether or not he wanted to continue studying healing. If he did, Vander said he would return to Wolfheart and apply to the Dawn Academy's Healing Arts School.

It saddened me to think of him leaving the forest. Wolfheart wasn't far, but with the demands of school and of my work, we'd be apart with little time to be with one another.

"I wish there was another way," Vander said. "So that we wouldn't have to be apart."

Vander was talented and had incredible dedication. His skills had grown so quickly during his time watching me, and I could see that he had great potential. The Dawn Academy's HAS was good, but he would go way further if he could study under a master bear healer like my father. If only that were a possibility, Vander would go so far. But I knew that my father would never agree to train him. He was a wolf, after all.

. . .

That night, I cooked the two pheasants I'd caught before we'd gone to Houndsville, along with some parsnips and carrots and boar stock gravy. The cabin filled with the succulent aroma of roasting pheasant and mingled with the warm smell of the fireplace. Vander sat on the bed, wrapped up in fur blankets as he watched me at prepare the vegetables. I couldn't think of a time when my little cabin had felt cozier.

Each bite of the pheasant was moist and bursting with flavor, the skin crackling with perfect crispiness. "My mother's recipe," I told Vander. "One of my favorites that she always would make during the festival. I haven't done it justice here, but..." I took a bite of pheasant, and wiped away some juice that dribbled down my chin. "It's not half bad."

"Tell me more about your parents," Vander said.

"Well, they're both healers. My mother studied to become a nurse at my grandfather's clinic. She met my father there, and they fell in love. Her real talent has always been cooking, though. She's definitely the best in Ursidcomb. At the Gathering, her food would always be the first to vanish. But she always made sure to make enough for everyone. My father taught me about healing from when I was just a baby, and my mom showed me how to cook. I don't think I'll ever be able to match her food, though. My father is a real taskmaster. Always had me studying and practicing. He was strict and uncompromising, but I owe my skills to him."

. . .

"I saw the book on your shelf," Vander said. "The Guide to the Bear Healing Arts. There's a photo of you in there with an older man. Is that your father?"

"Yeah, that's him," I said. "That was my grandfather's book. My dad studied from it when he was a cub, and passed it to me as a gift when I finished my studies." I smiled. "It's one of my most treasured belongings."

Vander reached out and put his hand on mine. "You miss them. Don't you?"

"We don't quite see eye to eye," I said, standing up to the clear the dishes. "And with my work, I haven't even had much time to think about think about them, much less miss them…"

"Pell," Vander said incredulously. "Be honest with me. You don't need to hide your feelings from me."

"I'm not," I protested. "I just…"

He gave me a look, and I could see I wasn't fooling anyone. I sighed. "It's been two years since I've seen them. I do miss them."

"Why don't you want to go back home to see them again?"

. . .

I shook my head. "They wouldn't want to see me. They made that clear."

"What happened?"

"I was supposed to inherit the family practice—I told you about that."

Vander nodded.

"At the end of their studies, Bear healers leave for a field training that typically last, at the most, five years, and then we return home. Usually, it's expected that they'll travel to neighboring bear towns. My first offense was that I decided to go Wolfheart. My parents are stubborn and old-fashioned, and were not pleased with the idea of me practicing on wolves, but they accepted it in the end. By year five, my mother was wondering why I hadn't come home to find a mate. My father was waiting for me to take over the practice. I'd decided, however, that I wasn't going to be coming home."

"That's when you started working for Dr. Elpaw?"

"Yeah. I experienced a drastic contrast of situations going from home, to Wolfheart, and then to Houndsville and the other towns. In Wolfheart I saw the level of healing practiced by wolf doctors, and I realized that it wasn't prejudice—bear healing was objectively more advanced. It was also my first time being in a big city, and seeing just how many people there were out there who needed my help. When I met Dr. Elpaw and saw the work she was doing, I realized that was what I wanted to do—help the people who could barely afford to get it. I wanted to use my skills for them. I didn't care about money or anything like that.

"The last time I visited home, I told my parents my plan. Both of them couldn't believe I was serious, but my father especially. He couldn't believe I would abandon the family practice. He refused, or was unable, to see past that. He couldn't see *why* I was doing what I was doing. He thought I'd abandoned my family and my home for the wolves. I was just trying to use my gifts to help more people. You know what he told me? He said, 'If you're going to walk out that door, and go through with your plan, you don't need to ever come back. Because the moment you leave, you're no longer a son of my mine.' So, I made my choice." I chuckled sadly. "That was during the Gathering, funny enough. Last one I ever celebrated."

I stood by the sink, the memories of that day burning through my mind. My father hadn't lost his temper, shouted, or anything like that. That wasn't his way—but his words and the disappointment on his face were far worse than any anger he could've shown. I believed very passionately that I was making the right choice, and so I went through with it, but that didn't mean it was an easy decision. I didn't think I could deal with seeing my father look at me that way again. I'd hoped he would see the greater picture, and understand that it wasn't my intention to abandon home at all. I wanted to open our home, to spread our skills out to the world. More people deserved our touch.

Of course, I missed them. I missed talking with my father. I missed the little bits of wisdom he always seemed to be able to give to me. I missed my mother's cooking. Hell, I even missed her way of nagging me. And I missed the time we spent together during the Gathering, the memories of being a little cub, curling up with my parents by the fire with our bellies full of my mother's delicious food, basking in each other's quiet and loving company.

I felt Vander's touch on my shoulder, bringing me out of my thoughts. He looked at me with such tender understanding, and it made my heart well up with love for him. He wrapped his arms around me, holding me close to him, and I held him back as tears started to tumble down my cheeks.

* * *

The next day, Vander and I made the journey to Pinetown to continue my rounds between the three clinics. As I expected, the place was overflowing with waiting patients who been unable to receive care during the snowstorm, which had put the few rotating volunteers that we had out of commission. The lobby bustled with crying babies, flushed faced elders, raspy coughs and people unable to fully shift back to their human form. Vander looked at me, his eyes wide, and I could see he was doing his best not to be overwhelmed.

. . .

"Ready to run with the pack for the first time?" I asked him. "I think you've learned enough to handle some basic stuff."

He nodded nervously. "Yeah, I'll give it my best shot."

I flipped through the forms and records of the waiting patients and set aside seven that I knew Vander could handle with no problem, and then two that would be more challenging. This would be a good chance for him to be tested. I knew that Vander had great strength and composure—after watching him in the trials it was obvious—but healing and working with sick patients was a different kind of pressure, and Vander needed to be exposed to it.

"Take these patients," I said.

His eyes widened. "Wait, alone?"

"I'll be there with you," I said. "Don't worry. Just trust your nose and what you've learned. I'm confident in you." I squeezed his arm and grinned at him.

"Okay," he said, his chest puffing up. "I can do this."

I had the nurse bring in the first patient, a woman complaining of a high fever and soreness. I introduced Vander as a healer in training who would be performing the examination. She seemed skeptical at first. It would be up to Vander to convince her that he would be trustworthy and competent.

"My name is Vander Luna," he said, shaking her hand. "I'll be taking care of you."

He asked her to describe how she was feeling, listening attentively. I was pleased to see how confident he was. If he had any uncertainty, he hid it perfectly. Vander had a natural energy and charisma, and I could see that it was quickly putting her at ease.

He's got great instincts, I thought as I watched him perform the examination. *He knew exactly what to say to make her feel comfortable with him, and he's asking her all the right questions.*

In the end, Vander determined it was wolf's chill, a common winter sickness. He wrote out a formula for medication and passed it to me for approval.

"Excellent," I told him, reading his measurements. "Have her take this to the pharmacist."

"How did I do?" Vander asked when she left the room.

. . .

"You're a natural," I told him. "But that was about as easy as they get. Ready for the next patient?"

"Send them in," he said eagerly.

Vander really was a natural. Even with the more stubborn patients, he was able to quickly put them at ease and win their confidence. He of course needed my help with the more difficult cases, but he was able to turn to me for assistance without the patients ever doubting his abilities. His easy charm was a powerful asset that was just as important as his absorptive mind.

Eventually, I let Vander handle some of the assistant duties on his own—basic checkups, helping the nurses mix medicine, greeting patients. I could see how eager he was to learn, how excited he was for a challenge, and watching him filled my heart with love and pride. I could see just how much potential he had. He would make a great healer.

After lunch, Helena arrived to take over at Pinetown, and Vander and I left for Forest Ridge. The situation there was similar—the clinic was packed with people waiting to be treated. Working alongside Vander, I felt our bond as a couple strengthening and my feelings for him deepening. I was not the type to get easily distracted from my job, but at times I found myself unable to resist admiring him as he worked. Vander was glowing brightly, and it was a joy to see him thrive.

. . .

"Who's the new guy?" one of the nurses asked me. "He's great."

"He's my boyfriend."

"Oh, I had no idea you were in a relationship, Doctor!" the nurse said. "Congratulations."

We worked until the early evening, and with Vander's assistance, our team managed to take care of every single patient waiting for help that day. Under a sky colored by the setting sun, Vander and I made the trek back home in our shifted forms.

"Everything alright?" I asked. He seemed to be lost in his thoughts.

"Yeah," he said. "I'm fine. Pell, have you ever had a moment when you realized everything in your life had changed?"

"Sure," I said. "It was the moment I fell in love with you."

Vander laughed in surprise. "Oh, really? When was that?"

I thought about it. "Honestly, um, it was after I performed the tongue treatment on you."

. . .

"Really?"

"I didn't recognize it as love at the time, but I was drawn to you in a way I've never been with anyone." I smiled shyly. "I just... am not good with those kinds of things. Feelings, and expressing them, and all of that. I think I wanted to believe that I didn't feel anything for you, because I knew you'd be moving on soon. Obviously, I wasn't able to fight my desires."

"One of us would've jumped the other eventually," he said. "I mean, after being licked like that? Phew. I was dying for more."

I chuckled and nuzzled up against him, and he affectionately nipped my ear.

"This entire ride with you has been nothing but amazing changes, one after the other," Vander said.

"When did you realize?" I asked. "That you were in love with me?"

"When you were fighting to save Rian," he said matter-of-factly. "That was when I knew for sure. Seeing you work, it was like I got a peek at your soul. You were amazing. Yeah, a lot changed for me at that moment. That was about when I realized that healing was calling to me. And today was when I realized that I'd absolutely made the right choice. Have you heard of battle flow, Pell?"

"No," I said.

"It's a state of mind that fighters achieve in the heat of battle. My brother, Loch, and my father would always talk about it. Loch would always say that was how he knew he was born to be a fighter—he could lose himself in the moment, relying purely on his instinct during a fight. When I was training for the FAS trials, I wondered when I would experience that feeling. I figured that I just wasn't skilled enough yet. That it'd come to me eventually. It never did."

"Until today," I said, and he nodded.

"It was an incredible feeling."

"I know what you're talking about. It's that moment of effortless concentration, where your mind and soul seem to come free from everything that'd been holding it down. Everything comes naturally, without fear or hesitation."

"I know that I made the right decision," Vander said. "There's no question about it in my mind—I was meant to study healing. And I was meant to be here with you."

VANDER

Over the following week, I continued to shadow Pell at the clinics, along with assisting the other doctors and nurses and occasionally taking my own patients. I sought out every opportunity I could to learn more about healing, to the point where I was sure that I was annoying some of the staff whom I pestered with constant questions when Pell wasn't around. The thing I quickly learned was that Pell was by far the most knowledgeable healer there, despite being much younger than everyone else. The only person who seemed to occasionally exceed his skill was Dr. Helena Elpaw, who was a top graduate of the HAS.

Back at the cabin, I read and re-read Pell's copy of the Guide to the Bear Healing Arts. Pell pulled out a few other books he had in storage, and I devoured them too. I'd always avoided reading during school, but now I couldn't get enough. That same "battle flow" I had working with patients had come to me during study.

. . .

Time flew by, and soon the Food Gathering festival was only a week away. It marked the end of winter, and the time when I could submit my application to the Healing Arts School for the upcoming season. That also meant that I would be leaving the forest, leaving Houndsville and the other towns, and leaving Pell.

I didn't want to have to be away from him, trapped in the city with my studies, but I also knew that I couldn't accept anything but the best education, and the HAS was the best available to wolfkind. I called my brother-in-law's father, Julius Croc, who was a master healer and a graduate of the HAS, to get advice about applying to the school.

"Because you were eligible to test for the FAS, you should have no problems being eligible for the HAS entrance exams. However, since your breadth of knowledge and preparation lay in the fighting arts, you may have difficulty passing the exam."

"I've been studying," I said. "I've been working as a volunteer with Dr. Helena Elpaw at her clinics."

Mr. Croc sounded surprised. "Is that right?"

"Do you know her?"

. . .

"She went to the HAS probably about ten years after I graduated. I've met her several times my work with the Academy. How did you come to meet her?"

"Through my boyfriend, Pell Darkclaw. He's—"

"Darkclaw? Of the Ursidcomb Darkclaws?"

"Yeah," I said. "You know them, Mr. Croc?"

"Not personally, only by reputation. The Darkclaws are incredibly skilled healers. From what I understand Cill Darkclaw—the father—operates his own clinic and school in Ursidcomb."

"Yes," I said. "That's right."

"Vander, have you considered studying at the Darkclaw clinic? As odd as this may sound, the education you'd receive there would rival what you could get at the HAS."

"No, Mr. Croc, that doesn't sound odd at all. I've been studying with Pell, learning what I can from him, and it's obvious even to someone as unexperienced as myself that his skills are above what's normal. But I don't think that's an option. From what Pell has told me, it doesn't seem like they would accept a wolf."

. . .

"The older generations can be very inclusive and wary of outsiders. Wolves included," said Mr. Croc. "However, it might worth a shot. The headmaster of the HAS invited Cill Darkclaw to guest lecture at the school. It may interest you to know that although he turned down the offer, Dr. Darkclaw has kept up friendly correspondence with the HAS. Over the last several months, he's contributed research and instructional materials for use at the school."

"Really?" I wondered if Pell knew about that, and realized that he probably didn't. He hadn't spoken to his father in two years, after all.

"Yes. I know that he's been contacted by us on several occasions in the past, but this was the first time he'd actually kept correspondence."

I thanked Mr. Croc for the information and hung up the phone.

If I could study healing in Ursidcomb, it'd mean being close to Pell, and receiving a top-notch education. I hadn't even considered it an option before, because of Pell's relationship with his parents and their apparent dislike of wolves. But if Pell's father had been working with the HAS recently... Maybe there was a possibility there.

. . .

Pell came back into the cabin with two small rabbits in his hands—he'd been out hunting dinner.

"Best I could find today," he said. "Not very exciting. I'm hoping that I can manage something better for the Gathering. Maybe a deer. Fish, young boar, turkey."

"That'll be quite a feast for two," I said.

"I haven't celebrated it in years. And it'll be your first time. It's gotta be right. We can bring the food to town and share it."

I smiled, and got up to help Pell by washing the vegetables as he cleaned the rabbits. "I've been thinking, Pell… Let's go to Ursidcomb for the Gathering."

He looked at me like I was crazy. "Ursidcomb?"

"I want to meet your parents. And I think you should see them again. You can't just leave your relationship with them like this. You need to have some kind of closure."

"I've had my closure. Dad made that very clear."

. . .

"It's been two years, though, two years to cool down and to think about things. To change. They're not getting younger. Pell, I think we should go."

"I know you do, but… I couldn't hear those words a second time. The memory hurts enough as it is."

"I know you're afraid," I said. "I understand. It's fine to be afraid. But I know you want to see them. I know you miss them."

Pell was silent and continued to clean the two rabbits. Blood streaked the sink. I turned back to my vegetables.

"Did you know your father has been communicating with the Dawn Academy's Healing Arts School over the past few months? He's been working with them."

He huffed. "Where'd you hear that?"

"My brother-in-law's father is a master healer from the HAS. He works there. I spoke with him just now to ask for advice about admissions. That's what he told me."

"He's mistaken," Pell said.

. . .

"Is your father named Cill?"

Pell stared at me, his mouth agape. "Yeah," he said. He shook his head. "Dad is working with the Dawn Academy. It has to be a mistake. I can't imagine him doing something like that."

"Mr. Croc told me that he contributed instructional materials and research."

Pell stared at the skinned rabbits in his hands. "I can't believe it."

"He… also suggested that I appeal to your father to study under him."

"You're kidding me."

"No. The more I think about it, the more it makes sense. I'll get a better education, and I'll be close to you."

Pell laughed in disbelief. "Even if he was open to teaching wolves, which I still can't believe, it's not like the HAS where you just apply. My father teaches only a small handful of students at a time, sometimes only one or two. That's just how it works with bears. A master takes an apprentice."

. . .

"Then... maybe you can teach me?"

"If I could, I would've made that offer to you already. But I'm still learning. I'm not a master healer. I'll probably never officially be one. It's up to my father to adorn me with that title."

"Then I'll go on my own," I said. "I'm going to try."

"You're going to go to Ursidcomb?"

"Yes."

"When?"

"As soon as I can," I said. "Tomorrow, even. I want you to come with me. I want you to see your parents again."

Pell shook his head. "I can't stop you if you want to go there. But I can't go. I'm sorry, Vander. I just can't do it."

I touched his shoulder. "Think about it," I said. "Please."

He continued cooking dinner in silence, and we ate in silence, too. I knew he wasn't upset at me, but it was obvious that what I'd told him was weighing heavily on his mind. I felt terrible to see him looking so dispirited, but I knew that I had to go. And even if his father rejected my request, I needed to let him and Pell's mother know that their son was doing work they should be proud of. I figured that with the Gathering around the corner, they might be more receptive to reuniting with Pell.

He needed it. I knew that despite how much he fought against it, and said that he didn't want to see them ever again, it was hurting him.

"I love you," I told him later that night. "I know that you don't want me to go, and I know it must feel like I'm betraying you in some way by going. But I have to."

The solemnness on his face cleared for the first time that evening. "No, Vander, it doesn't feel that way at all. I know why you want to go, and do support your decision. I just hope you can understand mine."

I nodded. "Yeah. I understand why you won't go, even though I don't agree with your decision."

He took my hand and kissed me. "I love you, too. You're the best thing that's ever happened to me." He sighed. "If fate brought us together, I'll trust fate. I'm sure everything will turn out. Even if you do have to go back to Wolfheart, we'll make things work."

. . .

"Yeah, I know we will."

* * *

The next day, I arranged with my family driver to come to take me to Ursidcomb from Houndsville. Pell had a shift at the clinic, so he accompanied me to town and was very adamant in making sure I knew that he supported my decision to go. I hoped that he would change his mind and decide to come with me, but he didn't, and I hadn't really expected him to. It was clear that the memories of what had happened were very painful for him. I hoped that at the very least, I could bring back some good news for him, or even just an update on his parents that might bring him some resolution and maybe even open the door to a reunion in the future.

I sat with Pell beneath a covered bus stop outside of the clinic, our shoulders resting against each other. He put his hand on my thigh and absently rubbed my leg as he stared off towards the mountains in the north. His touch sent tingles through my body, and I fought the urge to drag him inside to the clinic's staff room and have my way with him.

He smiled, and I could see that he was nervous. "Call me, and I can be back in town to meet you tonight."

"You really don't think I've got a shot, do you?"

"It's not you, it's just my dad. I think that he'd be an idiot not to take you as a student. But I know how he is…"

. . .

The car arrived a short while later, a black luxury sedan with tinted windows that was a glaring eyesore in a place like Houndsville. It was a weird little reminder of the world I'd come from, and suddenly the month I'd been gone felt like ages. The driver, Thomas, came out and opened the back door for me.

I gave Pell a hug. "Is there anything you want me to tell your parents?" I asked him.

Pell shook his head, no. "Nothing I haven't already told them."

I gave his hand a squeeze, and slid onto the leather seat. Thomas closed the door, and I watched Pell through the darkened window as we pulled away from the curb. With one hand pushed into his pocket, he gave me a final wave. I waved back, unsure if he could see me. I breathed out a long sigh. Surprisingly, I wasn't so nervous about going to Ursidcomb and meeting Pell's parents. I badly wanted this to work out, not just for my education, but because I really wanted to help Pell. I believed that there was a chance that they could come around. I *felt* it.

I'll trust fate. That's what he'd said to me. I had to trust that fate was the gut feeling that was pushing me to do this.

. . .

"Wonderful to see you again, sir," Thomas said from up front.

"You too, Thomas," I said. "How are things going back home?"

"As you might've heard, your elder brother, Christophe, has been causing some distress with your parents."

"*Christophe?*" I laughed. "Are you sure you don't mean Loch?" I couldn't imagine goody two paws, perfect son, top of the class, ace alpha Christophe Luna to be causing any distress with Mom and Dad.

"No, sir," Thomas said, a hint of amusement in his voice. "I mean Christophe. I'm surprised you haven't been filled in. I should keep my jaw shut, it's not my place to relate your family business."

"Oh, no, no. You tell me everything, Thomas. What's been happening?"

He cleared his throat and glanced at me through the rearview mirror. I could see the gleam in his yellow eyes that he was dying to fill me in. "Well, this only what I've heard in passing, so it may not be entirely accurate, understand?"

"I got it. I won't say a word that you told me, don't worry."

. . .

"From what I understand, Christophe has been seeing someone."

"Well, about damn time. Okay, go on. Who is this angelic person who could stand to be with my older brother, and why is it a big deal they're together?"

"Well, apparently, this omega who Christophe is enamored with recently got out of prison."

My mouth dropped open. "That is a big deal. Why were in they in jail? How did Christophe even meet this person?"

"I don't know," Thomas said. "Your parents would obviously not approve of the relationship, so Christophe left the Luna house. That happened about a few days ago. That's about all I know."

"Hounds of Hell," I muttered. "Well, at least I won't have to worry about them being on my back about anything for a while."

The drive went by quickly. Thomas pulled the car off the main road, and we passed by a snow covered sign that said "Ursidcomb, Home of A Hundred Honeys."

. . .

Trees surrounded us on every side, and another smaller sign further down had "Welcome to Bear Country" written on it in a fancy script. The road was neatly plowed of all snow, and was freshly paved and free of potholes, unlike the worn roads that ran through Houndsville. We soon passed by a large general store, a restaurant, and a hotel, all quaintly constructed from wood in the same style that Pell's cabin was. Everything seemed well maintained, and although the town was obviously very small, it was nothing like Houndsille or any of the forest border towns that Pell and I volunteered at. It reminded me of what Diamond Dust looked like in the photos I'd seen of it—clean and modern with a rustic feel. I could tell that the people here were pretty affluent types.

"Where would you like me to take you, sir?" Thomas asked.

"The Darkclaw Healing Clinic," I said.

We passed by a large, two story building, its red roof covered in snow. Its eaves were green, with delicate white paintings of bears, flowers and trees all along them. A large tarp sign was strung up above the door that said "Happy Food Gathering Festival!" A group of people stood out in front, chatting while three bear cubs ran and played in the snow.

The clinic was a few minutes away, and sat right next to an elegant house that I assumed was Pell's childhood home. Thomas pulled up front and parked the car.

. . .

"Would you like me to wait somewhere for you?" he asked.

"I'm planning on staying overnight," I said. "There's a hotel here, so I'll be fine. I might need you to come get me tomorrow."

"Hmm. Perhaps I should wait in Houndsville for word from you? In case the hotel gives you a problem."

"I don't think there will be a problem. I'll let you know when I need you. Thanks, Thomas."

I crunched up the snow to the front door, took a deep breath, and went inside.

The interior was cozy, with the same exposed rafters and woodwork I knew from Pell's cabin. Apparently, it was a bear architectural preference. The waiting room had a handful of waiting patients, and as I made my way up to the front counter, I heard some whispers and felt eyes on me. I looked around and saw a couple people trying to conceal that they were staring at me. Their looks didn't feel hostile, just curious. Wolves probably didn't come through town too often, other than to make a pit stop on the road to Diamond Dust.

"Can I help you?" asked the portly girl sitting behind the front desk.

. . .

"Hello," I said. "I'd like to know how I can meet Dr. Cill Darkclaw."

"Do you have an appointment with him?"

"No, I don't."

"I'm afraid that's the only way, with an appointment."

"Can I make an appointment with him today?"

She smiled politely. "Dr. Darkclaw is the master healer here. His schedule is very busy, and I'm afraid we only will accept wolf patients on a case by case basis. I can see if you are eligible to meet with one of our other healers for an examination."

"I need to meet with Dr. Darkclaw," I said. "I understand that he's busy, but... if you could please relay a message to him?"

"He's very busy," she protested.

. . .

"He'll want to know. Tell him, his son's mate wants to speak with him. My name is Vander Luna, I'll be staying at the hotel in town. Please tell him?"

She looked surprised and nodded with wide eyes.

"Thank you," I said, and left.

Saying I was mated to Pell was an exaggeration, but it'd just slipped out of my mouth. It probably was the best way to catch his attention, anyway.

Pell's mate.

I let out a wishful sigh and headed down the road, hoping that the receptionist would recognize the importance of delivering my message—and that Pell's father would care enough to respond.

The hotel was more like a lodge than a motel or inn like The Dog's Bark. It had a big communal living room with plush couches surrounding a roaring fireplace. Deer antlers lined the walls, along with still life oil paintings of succulent meats and banquet scenes. The communal spaces were mostly empty, except for a wolf shifter couple sitting on the couch and looking over a map. I found myself anxious and unable to do much except pace around my room as the time ticked by. In the evening, I went down to the dining room for dinner, and ate a startlingly delicious meal of braised lamb shanks that rivaled Pell's home cooking. It definitely wasn't something I would've expected to eat at a small roadside hotel.

Evening turned to night, and I wished that I'd had the foresight to bring one of the healing books with me. I tried to watch TV for a little while, but the noise became annoying and I turned it off. Instead, I ended up just lying on the bed, staring up at the ceiling while my brain went over all the crazy and amazing events that'd happened in my life over the past month.

What an adventure.

Suddenly, a loud knock on the door bolted me upright. I stuck my eye up to the peephole, and saw a severe looking older man with a grey beard standing outside. I could see the resemblance—it was Cill Darkclaw, Pell's father. I quickly opened the door.

"Dr. Darkclaw?" I asked.

He looked me up and down with a serious eye. "Are you Vander Luna?" he asked, his voice gruff. He reminded me of my dad.

"Yes, sir," I said. "Please, come in. Have a seat?"

. . .

"No, I think I'll stand. I won't be here for long. What's this business about you being Pell's mate?"

I smiled apologetically—maybe exaggerating the truth wasn't the best way to make a first impression.

"Actually, we're just in a relationship. We're not mated. I needed to make sure I got your attention, sir."

"Uh huh. So, you lied?"

"I wasn't going to take any chances. I needed to speak with you."

He spread his hands. "It must be rather important, then. Here I am. You've got," He looked at his watch. "five minutes of my time."

"Sir, I come from Wolfheart—"

"Obviously."

"—and I was training to enter the Dawn Academy's Fighting Art's School. That was how I met Pell. He saved my life, twice. Because of the storm, Pell and I were trapped together, and that's how we fell in love with—"

"You want to waste your five minutes explaining your love life to me?"

"Sir, Pell is an incredible healer. He's dedicated his life and his amazing skills to helping people who otherwise wouldn't have been able to afford to get help. You would be proud to see your son working. He's changed people's lives. I've decided to dedicate my life to becoming a healer like him. I want to learn from the best, and so that's why I've come here to ask for you to grant your son the title of master."

Dr. Darkclaw eyed me. "You do realize that traditionally, we don't share bear knowledge outside of the clans?"

I nodded. "I do. But I believe that you understand the value of breaking tradition in this case."

"Is that so?"

"Yeah. Dr. Julius Croc is my brother-in-law's father. He told me you've been working with the Healing Arts School. I don't think you'd do that unless you've decided that knowledge is worth sharing with others."

. . .

He let out a short sigh, the lines on his face softening. "So, tell me, Mr. Luna. Why is it my son did not come to speak to me about this himself?"

Hearing this surprised me. I would've thought he would know why Pell wasn't here—after all, he was the one who'd cut his son off.

"Dr. Darkclaw," I said. "I think you really should take a seat."

PELL

"Vander isn't working today?" Helena asked as I finished filling out some paperwork in the staff room.

"No," I said. "He's taking the next few days off. Sorry, I should've notified you."

"Everything alright?"

"Yeah, everything's fine," I said.

"You've got something on your mind," she said. "I can tell. What happened?"

. . .

"It's nothing, really," I lied. "Vander is planning on applying to study healing at the HAS."

"Oh, fantastic," Helena said. "Yes, it's important that he acts quickly. It's quite competitive, and the next season starts soon. So, he'll be moving back to Wolfheart, then? That'll be difficult for you both, won't it?"

"Well, the thing is, Vander is convinced that my father would take him on as student, so that he wouldn't need to move back home."

"Your father? In Ursidcomb? He doesn't teach outsiders, does he? He wouldn't even take in our overflow patients."

"That's what I told him. But he went to appeal to him anyway."

"Vander went to Ursidcomb?" she asked, surprised. "You know, you could've gone with him, Pell. You can take any days off you need, you put in so much of your time as it is…"

"I know, Helena. But you know why I don't want to go back there."

"Of course, I know the whole story, Pell. But isn't it about time you put it behind you? You're a brilliant healer, my friend, but you need to grow up and face your fears. Vander is there by himself, trying to convince *your* father to teach him."

"He knows what he's doing," I said. "And so do I."

Helena put her hands up. "Okay. He's doing this for the both of you, you know? It's not just for him."

Through the rest of the day I couldn't stop thinking about Vander. I could hardly concentrate on anything, wondering if he'd met my parents yet, and what could be happening. A horrible crushing feeling was weighing on me for letting him go on his own. I felt helpless and weak being unable to bring myself to face my parents again. The truth was that it wasn't even what my father had said two years ago that was making me feel this way. That hurt had mostly gone away. It was the fear of being rejected a second time that held me down and constantly gnawed at me.

When I got back to the cabin, I found myself unable to eat or sleep. What kind of alpha was I for letting him go there on his own?

I pulled the old copy of Guide to the Bear Healing Arts off the bookshelf and held its worn cover to my nose. Its warm aroma carried me back to Ursidcomb, to the home of my parents, and to the memories of studying with my father and finishing the day at the big oak dining table with a plate of my mother's amazing cooking. I opened the book to the first page and took out the photograph that was tucked away inside. I only wanted to make my parents proud, to do right by the values they instilled in me—to always help others.

Hadn't I accomplished that goal? Hadn't I done everything I'd set out to do, everything that my family would've wanted? I'd even fallen in love. And yet, I here I was, still afraid. Still feeling like I wasn't doing enough. Still feeling like I'd let my parents down.

This was the second time I'd been unable to face my fears and conquer my emotions, and now, I'd let Vander down again too. What was I doing? I'd let Vander go on his own to fight our battle—no, *my* battle. I was the one who should be fighting for him, who should be protecting him.

I shut the book, my heart churning with a new determination. I knew what I had to do, and I was far overdue to face it. People needed time to change—to get over fears or past traumas. Wounds took time to heal, and wounds of the heart and the mind were the most difficult to recover from. My wounds weren't healed, but I couldn't let that stop me any longer. I would do it for Vander. I would do it because I loved him.

Shifting into my bear form, I left my cabin and set out north as quickly as my paws could carry me through the snow pack.

***

By the time I reached the border of Ursidcomb, it was past dark and the town was quiet. I came out of the forest onto the main road for the first time in two years. Nothing had changed in that time, of course. Ursidcomb was a town where things didn't change. Sure, buildings got renovated. The old, buzzing and flickering streetlamps were replaced with bright new LEDs. Signs were occasionally repainted and refreshed. But the soul of the town felt the same as it did when I was a boy, and it probably had been that way for decades before that, too.

It felt odd to be back. The smell of this part of the forest brought me right back in time to when I was young, and I could see myself walking down these same snow-covered streets with my parents to the town hall, where the big communal banquet was held for the Gathering.

Even though it'd only been two years, I honestly hadn't expected to ever return.

I made my way down the main road, past Mr. Broadleaf's market where I used to go for honeycomb sticks as kid, past the Tellman's restaurant and the Salmon Lodge Inn, where a few windows were glowing with warm light. I stopped in front of the inn. There was a good chance that Vander was in one of those rooms—after all, the Salmon Lodge was the only hotel in town. I was going to go straight to my parent's house, but decided it would be better to see Vander first.

There was a good chance my father had refused to meet with him, so he probably needed my support.

Or maybe it was me that needed his support to face my parents again.

The man at the front desk was Mr. Jace Bledfur, the owner of the Salmon Lodge. He was snoring quietly, his cheek resting in the palm of his hand, his rectangle spectacles dangling off the tip of his nose. I walked up to the desk, and cleared my throat. When he didn't wake, I tapped the bell sitting on the counter. He snorted and nearly fell of his chair.

"Wha— Oh. Excuse me, welcome to the Salmon Lodge." He blinked and pushed his glasses up. "Pell? Pell Darkclaw?"

"Hello, Mr. Bledfur. I'm sorry to wake you."

He waved his hand, dismissing my apology. "I didn't know you were coming back to town! It's been a long a time. Back for the Gathering?"

"Seeing my parents," I said, wanting to avoid the subject and lengthy conversation. "Actually, the reason I'm here is because I'm trying to find someone. I'm pretty sure he has a room with you. Vander Luna?"

. . .

Mr. Bledfur adjusted his glasses again and fiddled around with his computer. "Ah, right. Yes, he checked in today. Room 204."

"Thank you, sir," I said.

"Wonderful to see you home, Pell."

I walked through the sitting area in the lobby and went up the stairs to the second floor. I was aching to see Vander's face again, and to feel him in my arms. Would he be upset with me? More importantly, had he spoken with my father? I knew that nothing that I could say to my father would convince him to let Vander study the Darkclaw healing arts, but I would try—for him.

I came to the door to room 204. I took a deep breath and knocked twice. What would I say to Vander? I didn't know. I just wanted to be with him.

After a moment, I knocked again on the door. The heavy sound of my knuckles on the wood shook out through the silent lodge, and I heard Mr. Bledfur grunt—he'd already fallen back to sleep. Maybe Vander was asleep. It wasn't extremely late, but he could've decided to turn in early with nothing else to do. I was pretty sure that he wouldn't have slept through my knocks, though. Vander was the kind of person who was always alert. I decided that if he was asleep, then I'd just have to wait until the next day to go see him. It would be perfect that way, anyway. We could go together to the clinic, and I could make introductions. That is, if my parents even agreed to see me…

I went back downstairs. Mr. Bledfur's cheek was back to its original position in the palm of his hand, his glasses dangling again. I was about to wake him, to ask if he could rent me a room for the night, when I stopped myself.

No, not tomorrow. I didn't need to wait for Vander to be there—that was just me coming up with an excuse to delay this thing. I needed to see them *now*. I needed to follow through with this.

After cinching my jacket tightly around my body, I stepped back out into the cold and turned up the street towards the clinic.

The way Vander made me feel was wild. I honestly could never have imagined myself feeling this way about another person, and yet here I was, head over paws for him. Being a healer, I couldn't help but take a diagnostic look at my feelings. The tightness in my chest, the burning urges I felt in my gut, and how it felt like I could hardly form a coherent thought about him, only that I wanted him and that I loved him so much, and that I couldn't imagine myself living without him.

. . .

What was love? A drug? No, love was more like an illness—a beautiful, painful illness that tore at the heart and mind in the best and worst ways. I finally understood what it meant to be love-sick. How many people really experienced love like this? Was it this intense for everyone?

To my surprise, I had the sudden realization that I wasn't feeling nervous at all. All of that fear and anxiety I'd had was just not there. As long as I was doing it for Vander, nothing could touch me, not even my parents.

Then, a crazy thought dawned on me.

I'm going to ask him to marry me. I'm going to ask him to be my mate.

How insane would that be? Married after a month together. It was probably the craziest idea I'd ever had, but it felt right. Fate had brought us together, after all. I wasn't going to ignore that.

I reached my old home. A brisk wind tugged at my jacket and whirled puffs of snow through the air. Somebody had made a snowbear out in front—maybe the neighborhood kids. The windows of the clinic were dark, but the lights inside the house were still on. As I made my way up to the front door, I caught the warm aroma of a honey apple pie wafting out from the house, mingling with the rich scent of lamb roast.

Mother was cooking, probably testing out recipes for the upcoming Gathering dinner.

The night before the big communal banquet, families held private dinners in their homes. The big banquet was a fun time to connect with the community and see friends, but the family gatherings had always been the best part of the festival for me. It was the one day where my family took a break from the stresses of the profession and just took time to enjoy each other's company.

I thought about how over the past two years, that family dinner must've been so lonely for my parents. I don't know why I'd never thought about it before. Maybe it was just from shame, and I didn't want to acknowledge how we all had hurt each other. The realization made me sad. And even though I'd refused to admit it and had buried myself in my work during the past Gatherings, I had missed it. I'd missed my parents.

"Here goes nothing," I whispered to myself, and knocked on the front door. A part of me expected there wouldn't be an answer. I was ready to turn away when I heard footsteps from inside. The little pinhole of light in the peephole went dark, and the deadbolt turned. I straightened up as the door swung open.

PELL

Even though it'd only been two years, my father looked so much older than I remembered. His face was creased and tired, his shoulders slouched. His once dark brown beard was mostly grey. His eyes, though, still held that same stern vigor that they always had. He looked up at me, his lips pursed in a flat expression.

"Dad—"

He turned around and walked inside, leaving the door open behind him. "Hurry up and come in," he said. "It's freezing out. What are you doing wearing a jacket like that? Should've shifted. Come on. You're lucky, there's hot supper still ready."

I stood there, just a little bit flabbergasted, and then followed him inside.

. . .

The house hadn't changed at all. The same family photos still hung on the walls where they'd been when I'd left. The photo of me after graduating from my training sat center on a bookshelf next to the other volumes of the Bear Healing Arts. The smell of dinner surrounded me, and my mouth started to water.

I followed my father through the house and towards the dining room, which was shared with the kitchen, and heard my mother's voice.

"Is it really him, Cill?"

"Yes, Vae, it's him."

She shrieked and came running out, and threw her arms around me. "Pell. Oh, my little cubby is home."

Stunned, I slowly wrapped my arms around her and returned the hug. She smelled of cinnamon, honey and baked apples, and just like my father, she looked quite a bit older than I remembered. She held me by my shoulders at arm's length and looked up at me with tearful eyes. "I'm so glad you're back," she said, her voice shaking. "I've been so worried about you. We both have."

. . .

She took my arm and guided me to the dining room. I stopped frozen when I saw who was sitting at the table across from my father.

Vander turned around to smile at me from his chair. "I knew you'd show up," he said. He stood up and came to me, taking my hands in his, and then kissed me gently on the lips. I was so shocked, I could only stand there, wide-eyed.

"You must be hungry, honey," Mom said. "Let me get you some roast, and we'll talk."

Vander helped me to a chair. "What is going *on?*" I asked, finally finding my voice.

"Listen, Pell," Dad said, shifting in his chair. He looked uncomfortable, like the words were refusing to come out of his throat. I'd seen my father give bad news to patients dozens and dozens of times, never with any problems. He was not the type of person to have trouble speaking his mind, so it was strange to see him acting so awkwardly. "I've... made some mistakes. I owe you an apology. Your mother and I do."

Mom came and sat down at the table, too.

. . .

"What you've been doing—your work—is important," he continued. "I understand that now. And I understand that I reacted harshly."

"Harshly? You practically disowned me, Dad. You told me not to come back."

I could see my mom's physical reaction when I said the word "disowned." She looked at my dad, and he rubbed his arm, looking pained.

"I know, Pell," he said softly. "And I've regretted saying those words to you ever since. I was just angry. I didn't get why you'd give up your family, your home, for outsiders. For wolves." He nodded to himself. "I've… I've learned a lot about myself since then. Done a lot of thinking."

"We both have," Mom said. "We can see that we were being very unreasonable."

"Yeah," I puffed. "I'll say."

"I finally understood what your mission is, son," Dad said. "I held a lot of unnecessary resentment in my heart, just because of the way I was taught."

. . .

"That's great, Dad," I said coldly. "So, you had all these realizations and you never thought to reach out to me?"

Mom held her hand to her face, and I could see she was trying to choke back tears. "I'm so sorry, honey," she said. "I thought about it every day. I was afraid to face you. I was ashamed about how we reacted." Dad's wrapped his arm around her shoulder, a gesture of tenderness I'd never seen from him before. He wore a tight expression on his face, and I realized that he also was trying not to cry. I could hardly believe what was happening.

"I think I was... just too damn proud to come to you." He held his hand up to cover his eyes. "I'm sorry, son." From below his wrinkled fingers, I could see tears rolling down my father's cheeks.

There'd always been a thorny net of brambles encasing my feelings towards my parents, causing me deep pain any time I came near it. It was something I'd accepted would be with me for the rest of my life, even with the incredible love I'd discovered for Vander. I'd told myself that I would work harder just to spite them, that I would never be able to forgive them.

As I sat there, looking at my parent's aged faces, tears wetting their cheeks, I suddenly felt the thorns release their hold, and I realized just how badly I'd wanted to hear them say those words to me. *I'm sorry*. As much as I'd told myself I'd never forgive them, deep down that was all I wanted.

. . .

I got up from my chair and wrapped my arms around them, hugging them close. "It's okay," I said. "Mom, Dad, it's okay. I love you."

"Oh, Pell," Mom sobbed. "I'm so sorry…"

Dad only nodded, his hand still covering his eyes as he cried. He squeezed my arm with his other hand, as if to say that he wasn't going to let me go again. I smiled, tears filling my eyes, and looked up at Vander. He grinned softly back at me, and I knew everything was going to be okay.

After our reunion and reconciliation, Mom brought me a plate of dinner while Dad left to go "get himself together." The lamb was incredibly delicious, and eating her food again, I felt warm and happy in a way that I'd forgotten. I was home. I was with my family again.

Vander sat adjacent to me, and touched his thigh under the table. He smiled at me.

"You need to fill me in on what happened," I said. "Because this is just too crazy."

. . .

"Vander spoke to your father," said Mom, coming back in from the kitchen and taking a seat at the table. "He left him a message at the clinic. We couldn't believe it."

"He said he was your mate." Dad walked back in and sat down, his voice back to its usual gruff self even if his eyes were still a little puffy from crying.

"My mate?" I looked at Vander, who shrugged sheepishly.

"I knew I had to say something to get Dr. Darkclaw's attention."

"Well, it worked," said Dad. "Frankly, I didn't think you were ever going to find someone at all. You were always so caught up in your studies. Vander tells me he has been training under you?"

"Not official training," I said quickly, unsure how my father was going to react. "Shadowing me."

"A wolf giving up fighting for healing," Dad said thoughtfully. He grunted to himself and shook his head. "Pell, do you know who Julius Croc is?"

. . .

I seemed to remember Helena mentioning that name before.
"The name sounds familiar. A healer from the Dawn Academy?"

"Yes. A quite prominent healer from the Healing Arts School. A wolf, of course. An omega. He's on the board of administrators. Very skilled."

I waited for him to add "for a wolf," but he didn't. Dad complimenting a wolf healer? These events were really too bizarre.

"I've been in communication with Dr. Croc at the academy," he went on. "I've learned that Vander's brother is Dr. Croc's son-in-law."

"Is that right?" I asked, and Vander nodded.

"Anyway," said Dad. "Over the past few months I've been working with the academy. Just basic things, mind you. Sharing some of my research and materials."

"You've been working with the Dawn Academy?" I asked, shocked.

"Well, I realized you were right, Pell. It doesn't make sense to keep our knowledge to ourselves, not these days." He reached out and put his hand on the back of mine. "Listen, son. I want to make a proposition to you, and I hope you'll hear out."

I waited silently for him to continue.

"I'd like to ask you again to take over the clinic."

"Dad..."

"But this time, I want you to do with it what you want. Open it up to whoever. It'd your place to run however you see fit. And before you answer—regardless of what decide, I want to grant you the rank of master healer. It's been long overdue."

My jaw hung open. "Dad, I... *Really?*"

"You deserved it back then."

With my father's blessing, I could open the place up to patients from Helena's clinics. I could rebuild the Darkclaw practice to take in people from all over—and as a master, I could train people. *I could train Vander.*

"Any way I want?" I asked.

. . .

"You're the master."

"Okay," I said, grinning. "Okay, it's a deal."

*　*　*

Vander and I were set up in my old bedroom, which my parents surprisingly hadn't touched since I'd last been home. I was stretched out on the bed, my hands folded behind my head as I recalled and replayed the night's events. It was certainly not how I thought things were going to go.

I was a ranked master now. I was going to take over the family clinic after all, and what's more—my father announced that he because his duties at home had been relieved, he was going to take an adjunct professor's position at the Healing Arts School. Absolutely bizarre—but I was beyond happy.

I knew exactly what I'd do, too. I'd bring in some of the volunteers from the three clinics and train them here—Vander included. With both my father and I sharing our knowledge, we could increase the quality of care throughout this region. The transition to bringing in wolf patients would take time, I knew that. Not every bear in town would see eye to eye with mine and my father's decisions. In fact, I knew many would question his sanity. It would take time for bears and wolves to warm up to one another, and that was fine. Ursidcomb would lead the way.

. . .

Vander had finished a shower and was drying his hair with a towel as he walked around my room in nothing but his underwear, inspecting the belongings on my shelves. "Reminds me of my room back home," he chuckled, inspecting a copy of Worldwide Shifter Biology. "Except in mine, every book had to do with fighting. Guess I'll be getting rid of those."

He draped the towel over the back of a chair and crawled onto the bed, kissing me on my forehead, nose, and then lips. I smiled and wrapped my arms around him.

"Huh," he said, resting his head against my chest. "I guess I'm going to need to find a place to live out here."

"You could continue to live with me," I suggested. "I'll probably move into town. Get something bigger than that tiny little cabin. Someplace we can study."

"I'd like that," he said, and he slipped a hand underneath my shirt and gently ran his fingers along my skin. I loved how he did that.

"I'll need a car, too," I mused. "With all the traveling between towns. I can't do it on foot anymore."

"I can help you with that," he said. "I'm sure my family would be happy to provide you with one."

. . .

"That wouldn't be necessary."

"They'd want to," he replied. "It might not be the bear way to take payment for things, but my parents will feel obligated to repay you for the training. They're not used to getting things for free."

"I'm training you because of your merit," I said. "There's no tuition…"

"I know," said Vander, "I know. But trust me, it'll make them feel better. And me too. Think of it as a gift, for all you've done."

"Vander, you've done far more for me. I know you spoke to my father. Something you said to him convinced him to change his mind."

Vander smiled and stroked my cheek with his palm. "No, actually. All I did was tell him how you felt. He'd already made these decisions a long time ago. He just couldn't bring himself to face you."

"I guess it runs in the family," I said. "But that's why I owe you. If you'd never come here… If we'd never *met*…"

. . .

Vander stopped my thought with a kiss. "If we hadn't met, I would be lost." His delicious lips pressed to mine, his fingers working their way through my hair as he slipped his hand behind my head. I melted into his kiss, pulling him closer to me. "I love you," he whispered.

"I love you too," I said. "You have no idea how crazy in love with you I am."

I felt his heat pressing against my thigh, and slipped my hand beneath the band of his underwear and took him into my hand. He moaned against my lips, his expression falling into a trance of pleasure. I flipped Vander onto his back and stripped off my shirt. He pushed down his underwear, revealing his hard excitement. I did the same. My heart pounded for him. I wanted to make him mine forever, and I could see in his eyes that he wanted it too. He pulled me in, kissing and chest and flicking his tongue across my nipples. My cock pulsed with want for him. I dropped my fingers down between his legs, beneath his soft pouch, and inserted them into his warmth. He moaned and begged me for more, his hands groping down to my length.

Vander stroked me as I fingered him, and I felt his opening pulse around me, signaling every wave of pleasure. I wanted to feel that around my cock, and I growled it into his ear.

"Fuck me," he whimpered. "I want to feel you inside of me. I want you raw."

. . .

There was no hesitation, no questioning. I wanted it too—not because I wanted to feel him without the intrusion of a condom, but because I *wanted him*. To finish inside of him, raw and unprotected, was to claim him as my forever mate. It was the ultimate act of bonding and love communicated in a way that words never could. I pushed his knees back to his shoulders. His cock dropped back against his stomach, and his entrance invited me in. I accepted.

"Oh, *fuck*," Vander moaned. I pushed my fingers into his mouth to quiet him. It felt naughty to be fucking him this way in my old bed, under my parent's roof.

I grabbed his thigh with my other hand and rocked into him, pushing all the way to the hilt. It was impossible for me to hold back a snarl of pleasure—he was incredibly tight, and without a condom, his silky wetness was almost too much for me to handle. Every thrust made my eyes flutter back as I did everything I could to keep myself under control.

The bed creaked with each one of my thrusts. So much for being silent—but at that point I really could care less. I was enraptured in our sex. Vander cried out as I fucked him deep, his gaze never leaving mine for one second. "You're going to make me come," he choked, grabbing my arms with both hands. "Oh, shit. Oh, shit."

There was no more control. My cock pushed in all the way, and the orgasm rocked over both of us at the exact same time, electrifying my body with a jolt of pure pleasure. I released into him. My cock throbbed, filling him up, spilling out every drop. Vander's mouth dropped open in wide amazement. "It's so warm," he gasped. "I can feel it…"

I slowly withdrew, and collapsed onto the bed next to him. Both of our bodies were quivering messes, and we held each other tightly as the waves of our climax continued to wash over us, like the rolling of water on a shore.

"I love you," I whispered to him, when I finally had my breath. He looked at me with exhausted eyes, his hair matted with sweat to his forehead, his cheeks completely flushed. I smiled and kissed him.

"I love you too," he breathed, and nuzzled up to my chest.

"Vander… I have a question."

"Yes?"

"Will you marry me?"

He laughed. "You don't even need to ask. Yes." He kissed me. "Of course, I will."

VANDER

It was the first time in Ursidcomb, at least from what anyone could remember, where wolves attended the Food Gathering—but to have a wedding on the same day was extremely celebrated and so any potential hard feelings were swallowed up by the overall excitement and happiness of the festivities. The community event took place in and outside the town hall on the main street. The street was closed, and tables and booths extended out from the building onto the road, with endless amounts of food, all the best I'd ever had in my life.

My parents were definitely not used to the rural feel of Ursidcomb and the loose and informal nature of the people who lived there, but it made me happy to see them doing their best to get along with everyone. My mom was a pretty damn good cook herself, as was my brother, Loch, and with the assistance of our house chef, the three of them worked to whip up several favorites from back home: fillet mignon wrapped in crackling bacon, roasted game hen and never-ending links of spicy, home-made sausages. I expected Mom to get competitive with Mrs. Darkclaw, but instead the two of them hit it off, and Mrs. Darkclaw took her around to meet and trade recipes with her friends.

At first, I couldn't quite tell if Dad and Dr. Darkclaw were getting along—they both were quiet and intense around each other—though Dr. Darkclaw did seem happy with Dad's gift of Wolfheart ale. Later on, after the ceremony, Pell and I found the two of them sitting at a table together, a nearly empty bottle of honey whiskey between them, red in the face and laughing their heads off about something.

After the first round of eating, the head of the town called for attention, and Pell and my wedding began. We took our vows up on the stage inside the town hall, in front of all of Ursidcomb, who cheered and shouted when Pell and I kissed. I learned how excited everyone was to have Pell come back—there was serious concern that the Darkclaw clinic would have to close, or would fall to someone less qualified once Dr. Darkclaw got too old to operate it. I did hear some murmurings of disappointment that Pell would be bringing in patients from the wolf towns, but those few complainers were quickly shot down and shushed by others.

It made me so happy to see my family mingling with Pell's, and with the community that I was excited to get to know. I'd been afraid that we would be rejected here, but for the most part people seemed curious to get to know us. Loch and Tresten's son played with the other kids, running around in their wolf and bear forms.

. . .

I wondered what Pell's and my child would be—a wolf or a bear.

"I was thinking about our child, and about who they'll take after," I told Pell that evening, as we snuggled up together in the bed of our new house, which had been built as a gift over the past several days after we'd announced our wedding. Seeing nearly the entire community come together to build such a beautiful house so quickly was amazing, and something you could never see in Wolfheart.

"Yeah?"

"I hope that they're a bear,"

"Why is that?" Pell asked.

"Because," I said. "That way he'll be an amazing healer."

"No matter what he is, he'll be an amazing healer. Or... maybe he'll be an amazing fighter. Or something else. Who knows? Whatever they want to be, I'll support it."

I smiled and nuzzled closer into his warm chest. What had I done to deserve such a wonderful mate?

. . .

He was a man who had lifted me up from the depths of hopelessness, when my life's path had completely vanished from in front of me. He'd saved me. He'd shown me the way, and shown me who I was. I loved him so much. Fate had brought us together. We were *meant* to be.

As I lay with my head on my husband's chest, listening to the steady sound of his breathing, I could see my path reappearing before me. Vander Darkclaw, master healer, husband and father. I was ready. And I would do it all with Pell by my side.

My destined. My mate.

Boy or girl?
Find out about Pell and Vander's child in the special FREE bonus chapter! Keep turning till the end of the book for the download link.

And if you enjoyed *Doctor to the Omega*, **please consider leaving a rating or review**. All positive encouragement is a great help to authors! You can easily access the product page by scanning the QR code with your phone.

NEXT IN THE SERIES...

A highborn alpha. A wanted omega. A prophecy of fate.

Highborn alpha Christophe Luna carries a paw print shaped birthmark prophesied to belong to the wolf he's fated to mate. After years of searching, Christophe has just about given up on the idea that fate could be real, until the day he sees the bloody paw print that matches his fated mate mark. The only problem is *who* that print belongs to—Mason

NEXT IN THE SERIES...

Arkentooth, the outlaw omega with a hatred for anyone highborn, who was caught breaking in to the Luna mansion.

The powerful attraction he feels towards Mason is undeniable, but to have a lowborn omega bear his children would be a disgrace to his family name. When he risks his family's reputation by bailing Mason out of prison, will Christophe learn that fated mates are just fantasy? After all, a lowborn criminal and a highborn heir could never *actually* fall in love... could they?

Marked to the Omega is a 45k word, mpreg story full of thrills, laughs and steamy romance, set in an exciting and vibrant new shifter world. It is the third book in the Luna Brothers Series, and can be read as a standalone novel. Approximate reading time: 4 hours - Perfect to curl up with for an evening of yummy M/M shifter romance!

Loch's story- Wed to the Omega
Christophe's Story - Marked to the Omega
Arthur's Story - Bound to the Omega

DADDY FROM FLAMES

Also From Ashe Moon

*"A surprising adventure and decisions affect more than one life and the town. Great story. **Absolutely wonderful characters.**"*

See why the Dragon Firefighters series has over 2500 positive ratings and is Ashe's most popular series yet!

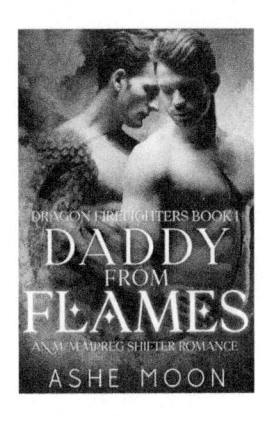

Pregnant and without an alpha, human omega Grayson must

rely on his tenacity to provide for his unborn daughter. But when a fire claims his home and everything he's struggled to work for, rescue comes in an unexpected form: the alpha dragon Altair and his flight of firefighters who reluctantly take Grayson into their custody.

Altair's resentment of humanity is matched by a conflicting sense of duty to protect the town they share and all who call it home, human or dragon. He and his flight brothers have never had to deal with an omega before—let alone a human—and now they have one living under their roof! Everything Altair thought he knew about humans, omegas, and mates is called into question—and with Grayson's baby on the way, he's about to find out what it's like to be a daddy.

Daddy From Flames is the first book in the Dragon Firefighters mpreg series. This book features dragon shifters, a human omega, firefighters, an industrial fantasy setting, pregnancy/birth, new dads, a cat, love healing wounds, action, fun, light drama, and, as always, a happily ever after.

KEEP IN TOUCH WITH ASHE

Stay updated with sales and new releases by subscribing to Ashe Moon's personal newsletter. Scan the QR code below with your phone camera!

* * *

If you're looking for something a little more personal you can also join my private Facebook group, **Ashe Moon's Ashetronauts**!

My group is a safe space to chat with me and other readers, and where I also do special exclusive giveaways and announcements. Hope to see you there!

FREE BONUS CHAPTER

Scan the QR code to sign up for my mailing list and receive the FREE bonus chapter to Doctor to the Omega!

FREE BONUS CHAPTER

First Edition Cover

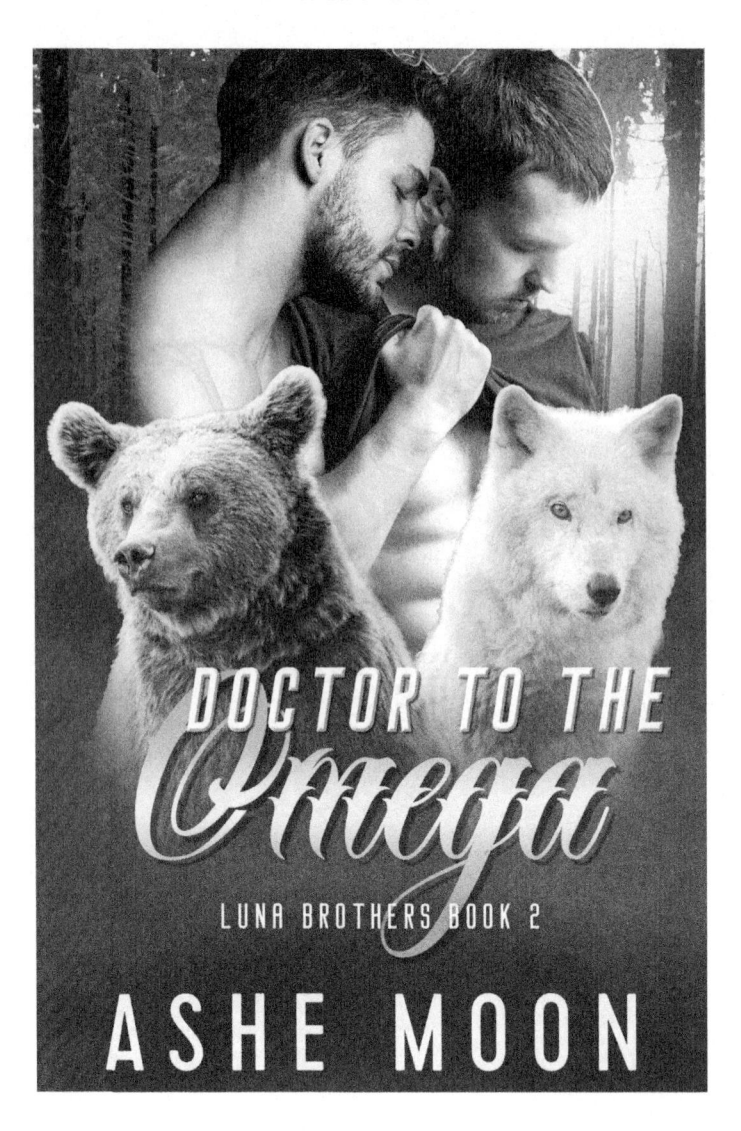

Printed in Great Britain
by Amazon